COUNTRY LIGHTNING

KING CREEK COWBOYS
BOOK 7

CHEYENNE MCCRAY

cheyennemccray.com

King Creek Cowboys

Country Lightning

Cheyenne McCray

1

The clerk scanned the form and handed it back to Jillian McLeod. "You filled it out incorrectly." She pushed another paper across the counter. "Go sit over there, fill out this one, and get back in line when you're finished." She leaned to the side and called out, "Next."

Jillian's scalp prickled, and she ground her teeth. This was the same woman who had "helped" her out when she'd filled out the licensing form when she first started getting ready to open her shop. Now, here it was, close to opening her dream business, and she'd been told her papers were not in good order.

She turned away, new form clenched in one hand, a stack of papers in her opposite arm. She was so angry, so focused, that she slammed into an immovable force and staggered backward, her papers flying out of her grip and floating toward the linoleum floor.

Strong arms caught her by her upper arms, keeping her from falling on her backside. She shot her gaze up to see warm, sable eyes and light brown hair peeking from beneath a dark brown cowboy hat.

Drop. Dead. Gorgeous.

He looked at her with a concerned gaze. "Are you all right, miss?"

Warmth crept up her neck. "S-sorry, I wasn't paying attention to where I was going."

"To be honest, I wasn't either." He smiled, and her belly quivered at the genuine interest she saw there.

Jillian ducked down to pick up her papers, but he crouched and reached them first. He stood, and she rose, and she had to tip her head back to meet his gaze. At five-four, she was the shortest of the McBride family, but she was used to tall men, and this one must have been at least a foot taller than her.

She took the papers he offered her. "Thank you."

"My pleasure, Miss." He held out his hand. "I'm James C. Jameson. Friends call me CJ." The name sounded familiar, but she was at an Arizona tax licensing office over fifty miles from home, so she had no idea why she thought she'd heard it before.

She took his hand, and tingles raced through her body. *Holy crap.* It really happened, just like the romance novels she'd read since she was a teenager. Heat flushed over her from head to toe. "I'm Jillian. Family calls me Jill, but to everyone else, I'm Jillian."

"Jillian is a beautiful name for a beautiful woman." His smile did crazy things to her belly.

She pulled her hand away and tucked her hair behind her ear. "I'd better figure this out and get this license form resubmitted before they close. I have a new business that hinges on it."

"Let me see if I can help you." He nodded toward the papers. "I have some experience with tax licensing."

"I'd love some help." She handed him the papers, glad for a few minutes more to talk to this sexy cowboy. "Thank you."

She had to hurry to keep up as he took the few long strides

to reach the blue plastic chairs along one wall. He waited for her to sit before he eased into the chair next to her.

His body heat radiated from where their shoulders touched. She shifted in her seat and straightened her skirt that hit just above her knees.

"You're a McLeod from King Creek?" He looked up from the papers and met her gaze. "I think you were just a kid last time I saw you."

Surprise caught her off guard. "How do you know me and my family?"

"I grew up with your older brothers—I went to school with Colt and Carter. Colt and I rodeoed together as juniors and seniors." He smiled. "What were you? Ten years old when Colt and I graduated?"

Her jaw dropped. "You're an old man?" At his amused look, she was afraid she'd just stuck her foot in her mouth like she did sometimes. "I'm sorry. My sisters and I call our oldest brothers that. You must be eight years older than me."

He gave her another sexy smile that made her toes curl. He had such beautiful eyes and was built long, lean, and muscular. "And now you're all grown up."

The look he gave her was one of a man appreciating a beautiful woman, and her face had to be cherry-red. She didn't think of herself as beautiful, but right then, she felt like it.

Before she could respond, he looked back at the paperwork. "I'd better help you with this before the place closes." He glanced up at her. "Got a pen?"

"Somewhere in here." She dug in her purse and finally found one. She handed it to him, and their fingers brushed. A little shiver went through her. Did he feel the same jolt that she had?

"I don't know why they're giving you a hard time." He went

through the forms in no time. "You only missed a couple of things."

She pointed to the stack. "And she said I had to fill out that other form."

He looked at the form and shook his head. "It's a form to correct the other form. Just more red tape." He reviewed it, checked a couple more boxes, and handed them to her. "Sign the bottom of that one, and you should be good to go."

Jillian blew out her breath. "Thank you." She got to her feet, and he joined her.

CJ nodded toward the window, where two women now stood. "I'll help you make sure everything is taken care of."

She got to her feet, and he joined her. "I'm sure you have more important things to do, CJ."

"Nah." He patted his back pocket where some rolled-up papers stuck out. "Already taken care of." They fell into step as they walked to the clerk's window. "I had to get my mom's ranch licenses put into my name."

They reached the back of the line, and she cocked her head. "I haven't seen you around town." She definitely would have remembered him.

"I've been in the service for the past twelve years." He shook his head and let out a long sigh. "Shattered both legs the day before my mom passed away, so I wasn't even able to make it to her funeral. Ended up being in rehab for nearly six months before I could get here."

"I'm sorry to hear that." She rested her hand on his forearm, his flesh warm beneath her touch. "Your mom must have been Mitsey Jameson."

He nodded. "Dad died a few years back, so it's just me."

Jillian let her hand drift away. "So, now the ranch is yours."

"Yep." He gestured for her to go forward. "You're up."

CJ accompanied her to the window. The woman looked sourly at her. "Did you get it right this time?"

Jillian was taken aback by her attitude. Something very rude nearly came out, but she bit it back in time. CJ gave the woman a winning smile. "I'm sure everything's in order now."

The woman turned her gaze on him. "And who are you?"

CJ settled his arm around her shoulders. "I'm Miss McLeod's fiancé."

Jillian shot her gaze to CJ, but he took the papers from her and presented them to the clerk.

The woman sniffed and reviewed the papers. She reached into her drawer, pulled out a stamp, and attacked each form with it. "One moment." The clerk slid off her stool and waddled to a copy machine, where she fed the pages through.

She lumbered back, handed the copies to Jillian then looked over her shoulder at the clock that said exactly 5:00 p.m.

Jillian sagged against CJ, then straightened in a hurry, his arm still around her shoulders. "Sorry." She stepped away from his casual hold. "Thank you."

He grinned at her. "Come on. I'll take you out for a burger."

Her belly flipped. "I, well, okay." She let him guide her out the door, which an employee locked behind them.

When they stood out on the sidewalk in front of the state office building, a strong breeze caught Jillian's long, dark hair, sending it into her face. She pushed it over her shoulders and stood facing CJ.

"I know of a great place in Tempe by the university." He inclined his head in that direction. "As for baseball, there are no spring training games tonight, and it's Arizona State University's spring break, so the place will probably not be crowded. It's called Home Plate."

"I've heard of it." She pulled out her phone and brought it up in her GPS. "Fifteen minutes to get there."

He touched the brim of his hat. "See you in a few."

Her heart skipped a beat as she strode toward her electric blue Ford Escape. She'd traded in her car for the SUV once she started working on opening her new business. She glanced over her shoulder and saw him at the door of a big yellow Dodge Ram truck. He cast a look at her and grinned, and she hurried to get into her own vehicle.

Once she was in the Escape, she followed CJ's truck out of downtown Phoenix and onto the freeway. She was able to keep up with him all the way to Tempe and Home Plate, so she didn't need her GPS. Parking wasn't too bad, which was unusual for the college town. She pulled her vehicle next to his in the lot behind the building and killed the engine.

It occurred to her that she didn't really know this man. She didn't remember him, which wasn't surprising. He was much older than her, and she'd been so young when he would have hung around with her oldest brothers.

During those days, she'd had her own little kid concerns, which revolved around Pretty Ponies and Barbie dolls. She hadn't been a tomboy like her sister, Haylee. She hadn't been athletic and a barrel racer like Leann. She'd been right in the middle.

Before Jillian even had a chance to open the door to her SUV, CJ was there, opening it for her. She grabbed her purse and took the hand he offered as he assisted her in climbing out of the vehicle.

She smiled at him. "Thank you."

He put his fingertips at the base of her spine, causing tingles where his touch pressed against her top. He escorted her around the building to the front door.

Spring weather in Phoenix was in the mid-to-high seventies, and today felt lovely. Cooler air swept over her when he opened the door to the restaurant, and they stepped inside.

True to CJ's statement, the place wasn't too busy for 5:30 on a Friday evening, with just a few other patrons in the main room and only two seated at the bar. Likely more people would show up as the hour grew later.

The relaxed atmosphere made it look like a great way to unwind after a long day—especially after spending time with a disagreeable county clerk.

He looked down at her as they waited for a hostess. "Would you like to sit at the bar or one of the high-tops?"

She considered his question. Sitting at the bar would be less intimate, which might be a good idea since she'd more-or-less just met him. She nodded in that direction. "The bar sounds good."

CJ took her hand and led her to the barstools. She climbed onto one of the black leather-covered stools, careful not to let her skirt slide up.

She crossed her legs at her knees as he seated himself. No more than a few inches separated them, and she was incredibly aware of his presence, and her belly fluttered.

He handed her one of the small menus set on the bar top. She took it and perused the limited offerings.

The bartender approached, a beefy woman with her hair thrown up in a messy ponytail. "What'll you have?"

Jillian pointed to the burger section on the menu. "I'd like the Arizona burger with cheese, curly fries, a glass of Riesling, and ice water."

"All right." The bartender turned to CJ. "And you?"

He set his menu on top of Jillian's. "Same, but with whatever domestic you have on tap."

"You've got it." The woman turned and entered their orders onto a tablet screen, which presumably sent them to the back.

Jillian turned her gaze to CJ, who was studying her. "So, Desert Blooms."

The warmth in his eyes eased her nervousness a bit—for a moment she wondered how he knew the name of her new business, then she realized he'd just helped her with her license —*duh*.

Excitement bubbled up inside her as she thought about her new business. "I officially open my shop and become a florist in a week, just in time for Easter."

The bartender returned with their drinks and plopped them down before retreating.

"Thanks." CJ picked up his mug and turned back to Jillian. "What did you do before?"

"I was an accountant for years but got laid off." She slid her fingers along the stem of her wine glass. "At first, I was worried about the future, but with encouragement from family and friends, I decided to pursue my dream of owning my own business. I cashed out half my 401K and got a business loan, and here I am, almost ready to open my doors."

He took a swallow of his beer and lowered it to the bar top. "That's admirable. Why a flower shop?"

"I've always had a green thumb." She paused to sip her wine and continued to hold the glass. "I was in horticulture in 4-H and grew dozens of house plants and had a rose garden." She sighed as she considered the future. "Next goal is to make enough money to buy my own house and have a rose garden like I did on my parents' ranch."

He picked up his mug again. "Why did you decide to be an accountant?"

"I was always into academics in high school." She shrugged. "I thought one day I'd like to have my own store, so I majored in business. I was fresh out of college and looking for a job when I applied for the accounting position." She blew out her breath. "Before I knew it, I had been there for years, and I guess it was comfortable working for someone else. Every now and then, I thought about owning my own business, like Haylee, but I guess I didn't have the courage to go it on my own until I lost my job."

"Takes a lot of guts to do what you're doing." He gave a slow nod. "Not many people have that kind of courage."

She smiled. "Thank you."

"Do you live alone, or do you have a roommate?" he asked before taking a swallow of his beer.

"I live with my sister, Leeann." Jillian shifted on her seat and tugged her dress closer to her knee. "Haylee lived with us until she married her husband, Tyson Donovan."

CJ lowered his mug and flashed a grin. "Tyson ran around with the younger McLeod boys."

"Yeah." She tapped her nails on the bar top. "Brady and Bear."

"A guy would have to watch his step dating a McLeod woman." He looked amused. "Facing five older brothers could be intimidating to a man."

Heat rose to her cheeks. "Let's just say they chased off a lot of boys while we were growing up."

His eyes seemed to darken a bit, a smoldering brown. "Just know that I'm not easily intimidated."

A full-scale flush swept over her, and she looked away, relieved to see the bartender arriving with their food. "Oh, good. I'm starving."

"Here you go." Light glinted off the woman's silver nameplate that Jillian hadn't noticed before, which read, *Cassie*. She set down two rolls of paper napkin-wrapped silverware, then placed a plate in front of Jill.

"Thank you, Cassie." Jillian set her wine glass down, smiling at the woman while refusing to look in CJ's direction. "This looks wonderful."

Cassie set CJ's plate in front of him. "Holler if you need anything."

"Will do." He pushed his beer mug to the side. "This'll hit the spot."

Jillian unrolled the silverware and put the napkin in her lap as she eyed the huge hamburger. "It's too big for my mouth." She picked it up with both hands. "But I'm always up for a challenge."

She took a big bite of the juicy and delicious burger. She felt ketchup roll down her chin, and she hurried to put the burger onto her plate as she chewed and swallowed the bite.

Before she could grab her napkin to wipe off the ketchup, CJ dabbed her chin with his own napkin. "There." He grinned. "Didn't want you to get ketchup on that pretty white blouse."

His touch left tingles behind.

She swallowed away a sudden burst of nervousness. "Thanks." She looked down at her silky button-up blouse, which had the top two buttons undone. It did expose her cleavage, but she didn't think it was too much. She met his gaze. "I usually don't wear white for good reason."

"Happy to be of service." He smiled and bit into his own burger.

Jillian ate a crisp, hot, curly fry and watched him from beneath her lashes. When his gaze returned to her, she reached for her Riesling.

CJ downed his bite with a healthy swallow of beer, emptying his mug.

The bartender asked him if he'd like another, and he nodded and thanked her.

Jillian ate more of her burger, curiosity about the man churning in her brain. When she had finished chewing, she turned to him. "How did you shatter your legs?" She took another bite.

"In a parachuting accident during a training exercise." He shook his head. "Ended my military career."

He ate a fry, and she swallowed her bite. "Which branch of the service were you in?"

"Air Force." He picked up another fry. "I was a Pararescue Specialist." He popped the fry into his mouth and accepted the beer the bartender handed him.

"That sounds intriguing." She cocked her head. "What kind of work did you do in that capacity?"

He swallowed, shrugged, and dabbed a fry in ketchup. "Rescue military personnel, like Airmen who go down in hostile territory. If they're injured, a Pararescue Specialist treats them."

"Sounds terrifying to me." Jillian shook her head. "I'm grateful to our servicemen and women for what you do to protect our country."

He smiled and studied her for a long moment. "You're much too beautiful to have been an accountant."

Heat rushed to her cheeks. His sudden switch in conversation, not to mention his compliment, threw her completely off. "Thank you." That sounded lame, so she followed it with, "What are accountants supposed to look like?"

His smile broadened. "Horn-rimmed glasses, for starters. The ones with neck chains."

She cocked an eyebrow. "I do wear glasses, sans the chain."

He smiled. "I bet you look just as gorgeous with them as you do without. Hell, you'd even look great with horned-rimmed specs."

She had never been complimented in the way CJ had been flattering her. She didn't consider herself the best judge of character, especially after having dated the world's biggest loser, Carl. But she didn't detect any disingenuousness in CJ. He seemed down-to-earth, honest, and sincere.

If CJ wanted to pursue something, she'd have to introduce him to Leeann—she was a fantastic judge of character.

As if reading her thoughts, CJ leaned in closer. "I'd be happy to talk to your big brothers if I have to because I want a chance to get to know you better."

Jillian's heart raced. She'd been gun-shy and hadn't dated anyone since Carl.

"I don't need my brothers' approval, and I'm old enough to make up my own mind," she said slowly. "I am interested in getting to know you better, too." She hesitated. "But I would like you to meet my sister, Leeann."

CJ studied her. "I want you to feel comfortable. We just met a couple of hours ago, and you don't know me well. It's been a long time since your brothers and I hung out. I'd be happy to meet up with anyone you'd like."

She decided to dive in. "I'm free tomorrow evening." Better yet, she didn't think Leeann had plans.

"Perfect." CJ's eyes lit up with his smile. He held out his hand. "Let me put my name and number in your phone, and you can call or text me your address when you're ready."

"All right." She pulled her cell phone out of her purse, opened her contacts app, and handed it to him.

He took the phone and focused on the screen, using both thumbs to enter the information before returning it to her.

She took it and slid it back into her purse. "You haven't had a chance to finish your burger."

He nodded to her plate. "Same goes for you. Curly fries aren't the best when they're cold."

"You have a point." She smiled and picked up her burger. It wasn't hot anymore, and it didn't seem as drippy.

As he ate his burger, she bit into her own and chewed. She picked up the glass of water the bartender had left for her and washed the bite down.

"This is one of the best burgers I've had." She held up a curly fry. "And these are awesome."

"You're right about the burgers," he said. "My fries are good, too."

They ate in companionable silence, thought after thought tumbling through Jillian's mind. She'd never met a cowboy as utterly sexy as CJ, and the fact that he was interested in her blew her away. She didn't think she was nearly as pretty as her beautiful sisters, but he made her feel that way.

Jillian wiped her fingers on her napkin and dabbed her mouth when she finished eating. She sipped her ice water and turned her attention to CJ.

He was watching her, a smile touching his lips. "Do you like baseball?"

"Love it." Jillian shifted on her barstool. "I've loved watching the Diamondbacks since I was a kid. They did awesome last year, making it to the World Series."

"Would you like to go to a game for our Saturday night date? I might have a couple of tickets." He smiled. "A friend has spring training season tickets and offered me his two seats for Saturday night since he'll be out of town. I'm sure they're great seats."

"I'd love to." She sat straighter on her stool. "I haven't been to a game in ages."

"Hopefully, they're still available. I'll let you know when you text." The bartender took their plates, and CJ turned his attention back to Jillian. "Are you ready to call it a night?"

"Yes." She nodded. "I've had a wonderful time, but I do need to get to work on my shop in the morning. There's so much to do before opening day."

The bartender plopped the tab on the counter, and CJ took it before Jillian could.

"I can pay half," she said.

He looked amused as he met her gaze. "You can't tell me that you don't know that a cowboy always pays. My mama raised me right."

She glanced at the ceiling before looking at CJ again. "Heaven save me from gentleman cowboys." She sighed and asked, even though she knew the answer, "Are you sure?"

He chuckled. "Darlin' don't even ask."

"All right." She smiled. "Thank you." Truth was, it was nice to be treated to dinner. As long as she'd been with Carl, they'd always split the bill. He definitely could have taken a lesson on being a gentleman from the cowboys she'd grown up with.

CJ put cash in the check holder and climbed off his stool. He took Jillian's hand and helped her to her feet. Her skirt slid up to her upper thighs, and she tugged it down with her free hand. If he did see, he pretended not to notice.

He released her hand, put his fingertips at her lower back again, and escorted her to her SUV. She used the fob to unlock the door, and he opened it for her.

"Thank you for rescuing me at the state office this afternoon and for dinner." Jillian tipped her head back. "I had a lovely time. At dinner, that is."

She made to get into her vehicle, and he took her hand and helped her inside. She wanted him to kiss her like crazy, but it was much too soon for that. She stuck the key in the ignition and turned on her SUV, lowering the window as he closed the door.

Jillian rested one hand on the steering wheel. "I'm looking forward to tomorrow."

"I am, too." He placed both hands on the doorframe. "Drive home safely."

"Same for you." She smiled and buzzed up the window.

He stepped back and slid his hands into his front pockets.

She felt a little flustered as he watched, so she took her time backing up, not wanting to crash into another car with him watching. Not that she wanted to, regardless.

When she was ready to drive out of the parking lot, she gave him a little wave and then pulled onto the street.

It wasn't until she was out of his sight that she finally relaxed. She felt giddy and had been on edge all night.

After her bad breakup with Carl, she'd been leery about dating for a while, but this cowboy chased away all her fears.

And she couldn't wait for tomorrow night.

2

Eight-thirty Saturday morning, Jillian perched on a ladder in her soon-to-be flower shop and swept her brush on the wall as she worked on the second coat. They were almost finished. The smell of wet paint hung in the air, and a cool spring breeze came through the front entrance where the door had been propped open.

She loaded sunshine-yellow paint on her brush again and slid it down the wall. She'd been doing a lot of the work herself to save money rather than hiring a professional paint crew.

Leeann had been doing what she could with the painting, fitting it in while working full-time as an X-ray tech, along with writing and preparing for her first book release around Christmas. Time that she normally allotted to making jewelry had been spent helping Jillian instead. She appreciated Leeann's help more than she could express.

Now, they were cutting it close with last-minute preparations —the store opened next weekend.

All her siblings and their parents had been jumping in to assist in various capacities, something she'd been incredibly grateful for. They'd all been so encouraging and helpful.

"There's a delivery truck out front." Leeann's voice came from behind her. "I think it's the additional coolers you ordered."

"Great." Jillian put the lid on the can, climbed down the ladder, and placed her paintbrush in a container of water by the wall. She wiped paint off her hands with an old rag and tossed it near the can.

Leeann planted her hands on her hips as she took in the walls. "The shop is looking terrific."

"Thanks to a whole lot of help from you and the rest of the McLeod crew." Jillian swept by Leeann as she headed for the door. "There's so much more to do."

"We'll make it happen." Leeann joined Jillian on the sidewalk, where two men unloaded the cases.

Jillian directed the men where to put them in the shop, and soon, a neat row lined one wall. She signed the delivery form, and the men left.

Leeann joined Jillian as she surveyed the cases. "Just think, soon they'll be filled with beautiful flowers from Maricopa County growers." She turned to Leeann. "It's really going to happen."

Leeann laughed. "We've been telling you ever since you got laid off that you would make it happen. And here you are."

Jillian smiled, and her gaze drifted over her new shop. A helium tank stood behind the counter near packages with a wide variety of balloons. On the left was a display of birthday candles, cake decorations, and boxed chocolates. A greeting card rack took up space to the right. She even had a small section of party supplies that locals would appreciate since they wouldn't have to make the trip to Phoenix.

The back looked like a craft room explosion with the basket and arrangement supplies. Haylee was an artist who used to own an event-planning business. She would make the baskets for Jillian's clients. She enjoyed creating them for fun and insisted on doing it at no charge.

Satisfied with how everything was going, she turned back to Leeann. Jillian opened her mouth to speak, but then her eyes widened, and she clapped her hand to her forehead. "I forgot to text CJ."

"The cute cowboy you told me about last night?" Leeann looked at her with amusement. "The same one I can't remember, either?"

Jillian frowned. "Is that bad?"

Leeann picked up a fresh paintbrush. "No, but maybe you should check with Carter or Colt, just to be on the safe side."

"I'll think about it." Jillian dug her cell out of her back pocket. "I just don't like the idea of asking our big brothers if they think I should date a man I'm interested in."

Leeann went to a ladder up against a spring-green wall catty-corner to the yellow one Jillian had been working on. "Don't think of it that way. Just ask one of them if they remember him."

"Maybe." Jillian's belly warmed as she found CJ's information in her phone, and she smiled to herself.

"I see that look on your face," Leeann called from across the room. "You've got it bad."

Jillian started a message to CJ. *Good morning. I'm looking forward to this evening. What time?*

She waited a moment, but no response came back as fast as she would have liked it to. She slid the phone into her back pocket, grabbed a fresh paintbrush, and climbed up the ladder.

The memory of CJ's killer smile made her belly warm as she thought about last night. Her smile faded a little when it occurred to her that he might have changed his mind.

She attacked the painting with more ferocity, causing yellow droplets to fly off and land on her T-shirt. *Stop it.* She'd always struggled with self-confidence, one reason why she'd stayed too long with Carl. She hadn't thought anyone else would pay the kind of attention he had to her.

When she found out he'd been seeing someone else, too, her self-confidence had plummeted even more.

But then here came CJ, who seemed genuinely interested in her and thought she was beautiful. Family and friends had told her she was—when she looked in the mirror, she disagreed. But then, she'd always been hyper-critical of herself.

They painted a while, Leeann humming and Jillian lost in her own thoughts.

King Creek's Spring Fling festival started next Saturday, and she anticipated getting more business with all the people who would be in town.

"I've got to go to the restroom." Leeann now stood at the foot of Jillian's ladder. She hadn't even noticed Leeann had stopped painting. "Be right back."

Jillian focused on her work, and the hair at her nape prickled. She felt like she was being watched.

She looked over her shoulder and dropped her paintbrush. It landed with a loud smack.

CJ stood in the open doorway, his shoulder hitched against the doorframe. He'd crossed his arms in front of his broad chest and wore a sexy grin.

Her mouth grew dry as she swept her gaze over the tall, well-muscled cowboy. "Uh, hi."

"Hello, beautiful." He didn't move.

"Give me a minute." She put the lid on the paint can and climbed down the ladder. She picked up the paintbrush from where it had left a yellow splat on the concrete floor and put the brush into the can of water. She picked up a rag and wiped her hands with it before tossing it back to the floor.

She sucked in her breath, then let it out slowly before she turned to face him again.

He pushed away from the doorframe and strode toward her. When he reached her, he smiled. "Hope you don't mind me stopping by while you're in the middle of working."

"Not at all." She slid her hands into her front pockets for something to do with them. "Are you in town for anything in particular?"

"I had to go to the hardware store for supplies for some repairs I have to make." He jutted his chin in the direction of the store, which was across the street, before meeting her gaze. "I saw the name of your shop and thought I'd answer your text in person."

"The sign just went up yesterday." She waved to the new cases, the front counter, and the display stands for greeting cards. "Welcome to my humble establishment." She shook her head. "There's so much to do before my grand opening."

"You'll do great." He pushed up his Stetson with one finger, and she got a better look at his gorgeous amber eyes. "I'll be your first customer."

She laughed. "That's what everyone in my family says."

CJ TOOK in the brunette beauty before him, enjoying the sweet sound of her laughter. Jillian looked so damned cute with yellow paint on her nose and cheek and her hair sticking out every which way from a messy bun. She wore paint-stained Levis and a grass-green T-shirt, also covered in yellow drops and smears.

He'd been glad to get her text. He was looking forward to spending more time with her.

"I talked with my buddy this morning, and he still has the tickets." He rocked back on his heels. "Is 4:00 p.m. all right to pick you up?"

Her coffee-brown eyes drew him in. "That should give me enough time to get home and get ready."

"Hello." A voice from the back caught his attention. A young woman, who looked enough like Jillian that they had to be related, walked toward them.

He touched the brim of his hat. "Good morning, miss."

She reached them, and Jillian spoke up. "CJ, this is my younger sister, Leeann." She turned to Leeann. "This is CJ, who I told you about last night."

CJ held out his hand. "A pleasure."

She smiled as she took his hand, her grip firm and her intelligent eyes appraising him. "Nice to meet you, CJ."

She released his hand. "So, is the game working out for this evening?"

"Yep." He gave a nod. "My friend came through. Jillian's gonna text me your address, and I'll be by at four."

"That will be fun for you both." She smiled again. "I have to be honest, I'm envious. I love baseball."

"Like my dad, I played for Arizona State before I went into the service." He glanced at Jillian. "I guess you could say it's in my blood."

"So, we're all ASU graduates," Jillian said. "Go, team."

CJ grinned. "I'd better get running. Got a lot to do on my ranch." He smiled at Jillian. "I'll see you later."

She drew her phone out of her back pocket. "I'll text you our address now so that I don't forget."

"Great." He touched the brim of his hat. "I'll catch you ladies later."

"See you," Jillian said, and Leeann gave a little wave.

CJ strode out of the shop, and his phone dinged as his boots hit the sidewalk. He pulled it out of the clip on his belt and saw that the text was indeed from Jillian.

He whistled as he headed to his truck, parked in front of the hardware store. The yellow paint job gleamed in the morning light. He had a hell of a lot to do to get his ranch up and running.

Jim Butcher, from Country Entertainment Corporation, had contacted CJ about buying his place to turn into a dude ranch. CJ had met the man through a buddy he'd served with in the Air Force.

Butcher had explained they needed a working operation, which they would transform to bring in people from across the country and the world. The man had flown in last week to examine and survey the property, which Butcher declared perfect for their needs. They were offering one hell of a big paycheck—CJ just had to get the ranch to where it had once been.

It was going to take some elbow grease and time, the best part of a year at least. That sonofabitch foreman, Bill Reynolds, who his mom had hired while she was sick, had supposedly been watching over the ranch for CJ. Instead, the bastard had sold off all the cattle, horses, and equipment and had robbed him blind.

Now he was starting from the ground up. After getting the traveling bug in the service, he'd planned on seeing more of the world, and the payout from the sale would be more than enough to keep him comfortable for the rest of his life.

The sale wasn't guaranteed, and CJ had considered ranching as a career, not just something to do until he sold it. Who knew how he'd feel about things in a year?

Fortunately, he'd done a good job of saving while he'd been in the service, and his mother had left him a chunk of change the foreman hadn't had access to. So, one way or another, he'd get the place back in business again.

Once CJ was in his truck and on the road, he started thinking about Jillian again. The way her clothing clung to the soft curves of her body, the tawny highlights in her dark brown hair, how her cheeks turned pink when she grew flustered.

This was a woman worth getting to know well, and that was exactly what he intended to do. He wasn't a patient man—if he saw something he wanted, he went for it.

Jillian, though—she was worth slowing down and taking time for.

He mentally shook his head. This woman was going to drive him crazy if he didn't get his mind where it should be, which at this moment was on his ranch. He had all evening to spend with her, and he was looking forward to it.

He focused on the turn onto the road leading to his home—his family's ranch was eleven miles outside of town, so it was only a fifteen-minute drive from King Creek.

The yard seemed lonely as he drove up to the house. No dog to run up to the car, no cattle in the pens, no horses in the corral. Everything was so damned empty and lonely. The foreman had hightailed it to who knew where after cleaning out the ranch. CJ had hired a PI, but so far, no luck. The bastard was long gone.

He parked in front of the two-story home he'd grown up in. It was in good repair but needed some work. He climbed out of the cab and opened the back door to grab the bag from the hardware store.

For a moment, he paused in the driveway, looking at the quiet emptiness around him. What had once been a thriving operation was completely gone. An overwhelming sense of responsibility weighted his shoulders as he took in the once prosperous ranch.

He gripped the bag and jogged up the steps to the front door —the handle was broken, the main reason he'd gone to the hardware store.

The screen squawked as he pulled it back and stepped in

through the open doorway. It took a moment for his eyes to adjust to the dim interior as he headed to the right of the stairs.

The older model refrigerator hummed loudly in the quiet kitchen. He grabbed a mason jar from the cabinet, got the pitcher of sun tea out of the fridge, and poured himself a glass. He leaned back against the counter and drank deeply before setting the jar on the counter.

He needed a dog for company, and a ranch should always have a dog. He'd have to ask around to find one that could work cattle and was good around horses.

Shortly after returning home, he'd meticulously examined the ranch's state and created a plan. He started by repairing fences and corrals with new tools he'd bought from the hardware store. He was finally satisfied with the security of the ranch's perimeter.

Next up, livestock.

CJ went down the hall to the office and switched on the light. He seated himself at the desk where his laptop sat, its screen dark. After setting aside his Stetson, he booted up the laptop and reviewed his calendar. Next week, he'd attend a livestock auction and start acquiring cattle.

He pulled out his phone and brought up his contacts. He hadn't talked with Carter McLeod in a dozen years. Carter had the most successful operation in the area, so he was the man to talk with. Not to mention, he was an old friend.

CJ pressed the number to call Carter. After a few rings, a familiar male voice said, "CJ Jameson, is that you?"

"I've been meaning to give you a call before now." CJ pushed his fingers through his hair. "How the hell have you been?"

Carter laughed. "Life is good and keeping busy. We should get together sometime soon."

"I'd like that." CJ leaned back in his chair. "I wanted to talk with you about a few things."

"I'm listening."

"I'm rebuilding the ranch from scratch." CJ skimmed over the details to give Carter an idea of what he was dealing with. "I'm going to the auction next week to start buying cattle. Before that, I need to find a couple of good horses. Do you have any you're selling, or do you know someone who might be?"

"I've got a two-year-old appaloosa that would do right by you." Carter paused. "Hold on a sec." Carter's voice sounded muffled as he talked with someone else, and then he returned. "The mare's name is Faith, and she's a pistol."

"She sounds perfect." CJ smiled. "Do you have time for me to see her this weekend?"

"Tomorrow morning is best," Carter said. "Are you free in the neighborhood of nine a.m.?"

"I am." CJ's chair squeaked as he shifted in it. "Would you know of a place where I could get a good cattle dog?"

"Bear would know, if anyone."

"That's right." CJ nodded. "I heard he's the local vet."

"Yep," Carter said. "He's the man to talk to. Do you have his number? I can text it to you."

"I'd appreciate that, and I'll give him a call." CJ hesitated. Carter would hear about it sooner or later, so CJ would rather be upfront. "I ran into Jillian at the state tax office yesterday. She had a problem with her license."

"She's opening up shop soon," Carter said.

"I'm taking her to a Diamondbacks game tonight."

Carter paused. "You're taking out my little sister?"

"She's a lovely young woman." CJ couldn't help a smile as he thought about her. "Just thought I'd mention it."

"So long as you remember, she's got five older brothers."

CJ laughed. "And two younger sisters, who are likely just as protective."

"You've got that right."

"I'll see you and Faith in the morning." CJ sat upright as he prepared to disconnect the call.

"Have a nice evening," Carter said. "And take care of my little sister."

CJ signed off, sat back in the chair again, and blew out his breath. He felt like he was walking on eggshells—he'd known the brothers well back in the day, but that had been over a decade ago, and things change.

His phone dinged. He looked down and saw it was a text from Carter with Bear's phone number. He texted back a quick, *Thanks.*

Well, now to call another one of Jillian's brothers.

His phone call with Bear was shorter. CJ didn't know Bear well, but he was a good man, like all the McLeod brothers. Bear gave him two numbers for reputable cattle dog breeders, one for Australian shepherds and the other for Border collies.

When he hung up with Bear, he called the Australian shepherd breeder and made an appointment for tomorrow, after he met with Carter and checked out the horse.

For now, he had to replace the front doorknob, then he had a date with Jillian. And he was sure looking forward to it.

3

CJ and Jillian arrived at Salt River Fields in plenty of time for the start of the Diamondbacks vs Colorado Rockies Cactus League game. The award-winning ballpark was the first spring training facility to be built on Native American lands.

Jillian was more excited about this baseball game than she had been about any other she'd ever been to, which had a whole lot to do with CJ rather than the game.

It was a beautiful March evening, but it was still early enough in the season that it would get chilly as the team played well into the night. Jillian wore a Sedona-red Diamondbacks team jacket over a long-sleeved black team T-shirt and Levis. She wore her hair in a long ponytail.

CJ looked as sexy as ever in a jean jacket over a red T-shirt and Wranglers, which fit his ass snugly. Jillian had had the opportunity to check it out on more than one occasion. He wore a black Diamondbacks ball cap instead of his Stetson.

The atmosphere was electric as they made their way into the stadium. CJ handed over the tickets at the gate.

He smiled down at her as they walked into the park. "Are you ready for some baseball?"

She grinned back at him. "You bet."

As CJ escorted her inside, she looked toward the field where players warmed up. The excitement in the air energized her, making her feel like she was buzzing with excitement from head to toe.

They made their way to their section, the noise growing louder. Smells of hot dogs, popcorn, and beer greeted her nose, and her stomach growled.

The stadium was packed with enthusiastic fans in a sea of red—it looked like it was going to be a full house.

"These are amazing seats." Jillian's eyes widened as she plopped into hers. "We're practically behind home plate."

"Rich told me they were some of the best in the house." CJ slid into the seat beside her. "He wasn't kidding."

"I've never been so close to the field, much less home plate." She watched a pitcher warm up with a catcher. The speed of the pitches amazed her.

She looked up at the clear blue above and the streaks of yellow and pink on the horizon as the sun lowered in the sky.

CJ leaned closer. "How does a hot dog and beer sound?"

"The greasier the better." She flashed him a grin. "There's nothing like a hot dog at a baseball game, and it's just about the only time I like to drink beer."

"I'll be right back." CJ got to his feet, eased past the two men on the right, and stepped into the aisle.

Jillian drank in the excitement and enthusiasm around her. She'd always loved baseball, while her brothers and Haylee were all big football fans. Only Leeann shared her passion for the game.

She couldn't help but admire how the men looked in their

uniforms, especially how they fit their backsides. CJ definitely gave that view a run for the money.

A group of rowdy young men behind their seats were overly loud above the noise of the crowd. She cast a glance over her shoulder and saw they wore fraternity jerseys and Arizona State University ballcaps. No doubt frat boys from ASU. She didn't think she'd mind their shouts and ridiculously lewd laughter as long as they didn't get too obnoxious. But it wouldn't damper her enjoyment of the game even if they did.

She turned her attention back to the field. A strong, cool breeze caressed her face, and flags around the park snapped in the wind.

CJ returned with two beers and two hotdogs and sat beside her again. He offered over her share, and she gratefully took them from him.

"I'm starving." She unwrapped her meal in her lap with one hand while she held the beer in the other. "I've been looking forward to a hot dog all day. Baseball games are the best place to eat them."

While waiting for the game to begin, they munched their meal and emptied their beer cups. The alcohol gave her a pleasantly warm feeling inside.

They stood for the National Anthem, and CJ took off his hat. With her hand over her heart, Jillian looked at the Stars and Stripes and listened to the powerful words. She didn't have the vocal range for the entire song, but she sang along anyway.

When the anthem was over, she cheered with the crowd and settled into her seat, and CJ put his hat on again and joined her.

She turned her gaze on him. "Batter up."

He grinned, then she focused on the field.

They became absorbed in the action, which started off at a fast pace, with the Rockies going down with three strikeouts in the top of the first inning.

The Diamondbacks were the home team. In the bottom of the first, the bases loaded, one of their star players hit a ball out into center field. The player for the Rockies dropped the ball, and it was a triple play, the batter making it to third base.

Jillian jumped up and cheered as loudly as the rowdy guys behind them. She looked over her shoulder at CJ. "Did you see that?"

He grinned and shouted, "Sure did," over the noise. "That was awesome."

She sat again, and CJ took her hand and squeezed it. The feel of his grip drew her attention from the game to him. His hand felt warm and comfortable over hers, and it sent tingles throughout her. She met his gaze, and he gave her a sexy little grin that made her tummy swoop.

The game continued with the Diamondbacks and the Rockies neck and neck. Jillian was up and down in her seat with every hit when the Diamondbacks were up to bat, or every catch when they were in the outfield.

She always found it thrilling to see the players up close and personal, and today was no exception, especially from their view behind home plate. She admired the sheer talent and athleticism of the players.

CJ's enthusiasm matched hers throughout the game, and she couldn't help but feel an even stronger attraction to him through their shared experience. She liked his easy-going, down-to-earth nature but also his passion as he immersed himself in the moment.

During the seventh-inning stretch, he bought popcorn and sodas, along with a large package of peanut M&Ms. The fresh air had stimulated her appetite, and she devoured her share.

Soon, the players were back on the field. It had grown chilly, and she was glad for her jacket. CJ warmed her even more when he draped his arm around her shoulders.

At the top of the ninth, Diamondbacks led by four. The Rockies had the bases loaded with what could be the tying runs.

The next batter hit a pop fly for an easy out and the win.

Jillian and CJ jumped to their feet, clapping and shouting as the fans erupted into cheers, the music pounding out along with the enthusiastic crowd. Jillian bounced up and down on her toes as she applauded. CJ let out a whistle, and she grinned up at him.

They high-fived the frat boys, and Jillian laughed at their enthusiasm.

Her heart pounded, and her blood sang. "This was the best game I've seen in a long time."

She faced him, and he rested one hand on her hip. "I agree, and I've never enjoyed a game more, and that's because I've spent it with you."

Warmth flushed over her, beyond the perspiration rolling down the center of her spine from jumping up and down with the thrill of the game.

"I feel the same way." She smiled. "Your company made all the difference."

They made their way out of the stadium, the energy of the game following them into the parking lot lit by streetlights.

CJ shortened his strides so that she could keep up with him. "I've had a wonderful time."

He rested his arm around her shoulders. "Do you want to stop somewhere for a drink, or do you need to get home?"

She didn't want the night to end.

"I'm ready for more." She leaned into his side. "What do you say to going back to King Creek to Mickey's?"

He smiled down at her and squeezed her lightly to him. "Great idea."

CJ helped her into his truck and then jogged around the

front to climb into his own side. The engine came to life, and they set off for King Creek.

They chatted about the game, going over the plays.

She cut her gaze to him, her ponytail falling over her shoulder to rest above her breast. "I'm thoroughly spoiled now by our great view."

"We'll have to do it again." He kept his gaze focused on the highway leading to their hometown. He glanced at her and smiled. "Not sure about getting seats that good next time."

"I'd love that." She grinned. "I can live with sitting anywhere in the stands."

It wasn't too far back to King Creek. The drive went by quickly with their nonstop chatter, still hyped with excitement from the game.

He pulled the truck into the parking lot of Mickey's Bar & Grill.

"We're here already?" She looked at the entrance to the bar. "That went by fast."

CJ opened his door, and country music poured in. "Sounds like it's hopping."

She waited for him to open her door and took his hand as he helped her out. She loved the feel of his hand wrapped around hers.

A little voice at the back of her mind tried to interfere with her enjoyment, telling her it wouldn't last. He couldn't be as wonderful as she thought he was—she had such a bad record in the character judgment department that she should probably pull back some.

She pushed those thoughts aside for now, determined to have fun the rest of the night.

It occurred to her for the first time that they might run into any number of her family members. It probably wasn't the best place to get in any alone time with CJ. But, maybe that was a good thing.

He escorted her to the entrance, his hand on her jacket, pressing against her lower back. She loved how he did that, escorting her with a firm touch.

She saw a couple of people she knew. She didn't pause to chat, instead giving a little wave, and CJ nodded in greeting.

Two couples stood by the railings on either side of the porch. Music pounded from inside the walls, and when CJ opened the door, a loud but catchy tune met them.

"Oh, good." She smiled at CJ. "A live band. I forgot there would be one since it's Saturday night." She gestured to the two men and two women performing on the small stage across the room. "Desert Stars is one of my favorite bands."

"I haven't been in Mickey's since I returned from the service." He appeared interested as he looked at the band. "I've never heard this band, but they're good."

"It's too hot in here for a jacket." She shrugged out of it, and CJ helped her. He held it over his arm.

The room, which was hot from all the bodies in the packed bar, was filled with the scents of hamburgers, fries, and beer.

Jillian spotted her sister, Haylee, and Tyson at a table for four with two empty seats.

She tugged at CJ's hand and nodded in their direction. "We can sit with my sister and her husband."

He smiled. "Lead the way."

She moved in front of him, and he followed her to the table. When they reached it, Haylee and Tyson stood.

After Jillian hugged her sister, she turned to CJ. "You might not remember my baby sister, Haylee, or her husband, Tyson Donovan."

She turned to the pair and gestured to CJ. "This is CJ Jameson, who used to hang out with Carter and Colt when we were kids."

CJ held out his hand. "It's a pleasure, Haylee. You were just a little thing the last time I saw you."

She took his hand and smiled. "I don't remember you, but if you were in school with our oldest brothers, I'm not surprised."

Haylee released her grip, and CJ turned to Tyson and shook his hand. "You were friends with the younger McLeod boys. It's good to see you."

Tyson smiled, his brilliant blue eyes crinkling at the corners. "Been a long time."

CJ pulled out Jillian's chair for her as Tyson and Haylee sat. CJ took off his jacket before putting his and Jillian's on the back of their chairs. He sat and scooted up to the table.

The server, Janice, swept in and gave a couple of menus to CJ and Jillian before asking what they'd like to drink. They both ordered a beer, and she left them to make their meal selections.

"We had hotdogs at the park, but that was ages ago." Jillian set her menu to the side. "I know what I want. I've been dying for a plate of their nachos."

CJ skimmed his and set it down. "Chili fries for me."

Haylee folded her arms on the surface and leaned forward. "Leeann called to chat and told me you two were going to a spring training game."

Jillian wasn't surprised Leeann had filled Haylee in. She would have been more surprised if she hadn't.

"The game was fantastic." Jillian grinned. "The Diamondbacks pulled off a great win."

"They should have a good year during the regular season." CJ took off his ball cap and ruffled his hair before putting it on again. "They're sure looking good already."

"Haylee and Tyson went to Europe for their honeymoon several months ago," Jillian said. "I'm in complete envy."

"It was wooonderful." Haylee gave a sigh of pleasure. "It was the best trip of my life."

"Of ours." Tyson put his arm around Haylee's shoulder. "It was pretty damned incredible."

The server returned and took their orders. Jillian had known Janice since she started at Mickey's.

When Janice left, Haylee chatted about their time in London and Paris, and their cruise down the River Seine. Jillian had heard most of it before but didn't mind listening again. Her sister was so excited, so bubbly about it still, even though they came back months ago.

Jillian asked her questions about things she didn't remember Haylee talking about before. Her sister was delighted to share more, and Tyson put in his two cents.

When there was a lull in the conversation, Jillian said, "CJ just got out of the service."

"What branch?" Tyson asked.

The server returned with their beers, giving Jillian hers and CJ taking his before he answered. "I served in the Air Force for the past twelve years."

Tyson looked at CJ with interest. "I was an MP in the Army for a couple of years, then came back to go into ranching."

Haylee cocked her head. "What did you do in the service, CJ?"

"I was a Pararescue Specialist." CJ shrugged. "A parachuting accident ended my military career, so that's how I ended up in King Creek again."

"Welcome back." Haylee smiled at CJ, and he returned it.

She turned to Jillian. "How's everything going at the shop?"

Jillian groaned. "I'm excited about opening day, but at the same time, I'm scared to death."

"The store will be so successful." Haylee's eyes sparkled. "King Creek has needed a florist forever."

"I'm hoping our town can support a flower shop." Jillian couldn't help but feel a nervous flutter in her belly. "Although I did some market research, and with customers from surrounding towns, I think it can take off."

"It will." Tyson's affirmation boosted Jillian's confidence. He had a thriving ranch and another LLC as well. "King Creek's residents are known for supporting local businesses."

"Tyson should know." Haylee smiled at her husband. "The jerky company he purchased last year has been growing like crazy."

"That has a lot to do with local and regional buyers." He looked at Jillian. "From everything I know about you, Jillian you can take your business far, no doubt about it."

Her heart palpitated from an overwhelming combination of excitement and fear, which had pretty much been how she'd felt since she made the decision to start her own business.

The band struck up their version of a popular Kade Fields slow tune. Tyson pushed back his chair and held out his hand to Haylee. "Hon, they're playing our song."

She smiled up at him, her face shining with the love she felt for her husband, and Jillian felt a twinge of envy, along with happiness that her sister had found someone she loved. Haylee took his hand, and he drew her to her feet.

Tyson looked from Jillian to CJ. "Excuse us."

CJ raised his beer in acknowledgment, and Jillian smiled. CJ knocked back the rest of his drink and thumped the bottle on the tabletop.

As the pair disappeared onto the dance floor crowd, Janice returned with their meals. "Sorry for the delay." She set a plate of nachos in front of Jillian and gave the chili fries to CJ. "This band packs them in." She took CJ's empty bottle and eyed Jill's, which was half full. "Are you ready for another?"

"Yes, ma'am." CJ gave a nod. "Thank you kindly."

"Still working on mine," Jillian said.

"Be right back." Janice made her way to the bar.

Jillian scooped a bit of barbacoa beef, refried beans, and salsa onto a chip and popped it into her mouth. She crunched and gave a satisfied sigh when she finished the bite. "This is my favorite thing to order here."

CJ looked like he was enjoying his chili fries. "Good stuff."

They devoured their food, and CJ pushed away his empty plate while Jillian was still working on hers. She pointed to her nachos. "There's too much for me to finish. Help a girl out."

He chuckled. "Don't mind if I do." He put some on his plate and started in on them.

"Tell me about your ranch." Jillian studied CJ. "I imagine you have cattle and horses."

CJ let out a long breath, his expression clouding. "That's what *should* be on my place." He shook his head. "Mom hired a foreman to take care of business while she was ill. He took her to the cleaners instead."

Jillian's eyes widened. "What happened?"

CJ's mouth tightened into a thin line. "He sold off all the assets, from livestock to ranching equipment, and pocketed the proceeds. Thankfully, he didn't have access to Mom's bank accounts, or likely that would all be gone, too."

"That's terrible." Jillian studied his darkened eyes. "I'm so sorry to hear that."

He blew out his breath again and shook his head. "I hired a private investigator to track him down, but no luck. He's long gone. Probably living it up in Cancun."

She placed her hand over his on the tabletop. "I'm sorry," she said again.

His expression relaxed. "I never could back down from a challenge, so I'm ready to work my ass off to get my ranch up and running again." He grimaced. "Pardon my language."

Jillian grinned. "You don't grow up with a houseful of men without hearing your share of cuss words. Don't worry about it —there's probably nothing that would come out of your mouth that I haven't heard before."

He flashed her a smile. "I'll do my best to curb my language."

"What's next?" She cocked her head. "For your ranch, I mean."

He raised his ballcap and pushed his fingers through his hair before tugging his hat on again. "I'm looking into buying a couple of horses to start with, and I'll be visiting auctions to build my herd." He leaned back in his chair. "I chatted with Carter last night, and I'm meeting with him tomorrow to take a look at one of his mares. Bear gave me a couple of breeder names, so I'm checking out some Australian shepherd puppies after I leave Carter's place."

"Puppies?" Jillian perked up. "Aussie puppies are so cute."

He held her gaze. "It would be great to have you come along if you'd like to go with me."

"I'd love to." She beamed. "One of these days, when I have a house of my own, I'd like to get a dog. I was thinking of visiting rescue shelters."

He nodded. "That's a good option. A cattle dog is not likely to be found at a rescue shelter, so I'm going with a breeder, and it would be difficult to train most rescues to herd cattle."

"I think you're right." Jillian smiled. "I might start with a cat first since they tend to be more independent. I'll know when the time comes." She considered it for a moment. "Although, with owning my own business, I could bring a well-trained dog to work with me."

CJ gave a nod. "I told Carter I'd be at his place at 9:00 a.m., so I'd like to pick you up around 8:40."

"Sounds good to me." She looked at Haylee, who was starting a two-step dance with Tyson.

Jillian glanced back at CJ, who pushed back his chair and stood. He held out his hand. "Would you like to dance?"

"Yes." She got to her feet, slid her hand into his, and he led her onto the floor.

They two-stepped to the lively tune, Jillian thoroughly enjoying herself. CJ was a great dancer, but she could hold her own.

By the time they finished their second fast-paced dance, Jillian was out of breath and laughing from the sheer fun of it.

A slow tune started up, and CJ took both her hands in his. "One more?"

She tipped her head back to meet his gaze. He was so very tall and so darn good-looking. "Yes."

He brought her into his arms, and she slid her hands to his shoulders. He kept just enough distance between their bodies to be a gentleman.

They moved in a slow circle, and she felt his heat despite the inches between them. *Screw this,* went through her mind, and she fitted her body against his.

He made a low, throaty sound and settled his chin on the top of her head as he wrapped his arms more securely around her. She rested her head on his chest and sighed. It felt so perfect being in his embrace as she inhaled his earthy scent into her lungs.

A sigh of pleasure escaped her, and she smiled to herself.

Too soon, the song ended, but CJ didn't release her right away. When he did, she tipped her head back, and he gave her a slow, sexy grin that stole her breath. She swallowed, and he took her by the hand and led her back to their table.

Tyson helped Haylee into her coat as Jillian and CJ arrived.

Haylee pulled her hair out of the collar. "I'm beat. We're heading home." She hugged Jillian and whispered into her ear. "I like him."

"Me, too." Jillian hugged her back. "Good night."

Tyson told them both good night, and then he escorted Haylee through the front entrance.

Jillian looked at CJ and smiled. "It's been a long day."

He nodded. "I'll get you home so you can climb into bed."

CJ took cash from his wallet and handed it to their server with the bill. Jillian watched the play of his muscles in his forearm and wondered how the rest of him looked—totally yummy, no doubt.

He grabbed Jillian's jacket off the back of her chair and held it up so that she could slip into it. She loved the confidence in his motions. He put on his own, then gripped her hand and led her out of the bar.

The night air caused her to shiver, and he draped his arm around her shoulders. She wasn't sure if it was that or just being so close to him that warmed her. Gravel crunched beneath their shoes as they walked toward his truck, which glowed beneath the parking lot light.

He paused behind the truck and looked up at the stars, and she did as well. "I missed seeing the stars like you can in King Creek."

A shooting star blazed a trail across the sky before winking out. He reached for her hand and gripped it. "Make a wish."

She continued staring up at the sky, wondering what she should wish for. She was achieving a dream and opening her own flower shop. She had a wonderful family and felt blessed to have overall had a good life.

"I wish for my business to get off to a great start." She cut her gaze from the sky to him. "I really don't need anything else. It's not perfect, but I have a great life."

He rested his arm around her shoulders again. "From what I've gotten to know about you, I have a good feeling that your wish is bound to come true."

Jillian studied his strong features. "What did you wish for?"

CJ shifted his attention back to the sky. "I'd like to get my ranch operational again. But it's going to take a lot more than a wish to make that happen."

"If anyone can do it, you can." She was more certain of that than she could explain.

"I'd like to think you're right." He squeezed her to him. "Let's get you out of the cold, and I'll take you home."

He helped her into the truck, then got in his side and started the engine. Once they were on the road, he reached for her hand and gripped it on the center console. It wasn't far to her home, and it was a quiet, comfortable silence between them.

When they reached her home and he had helped her out, they walked past the bicycle mailbox Haylee had made an age ago and headed up the steps. The stairs and porch creaked in the otherwise silent night.

When they stood in front of her door, she turned to face him. "Would you like to come in? Leeann's home, but she wouldn't mind."

He gave a slow shake of his head. "It's late, and I'd better let you get to bed." He reached up and brushed hair from her cheek. "I had a great time with you."

Words stuck in her throat, but she finally got them out. "I enjoyed myself, too."

He pressed his lips to her forehead, and she caught her breath. He looked into her eyes. "I'll see you in the morning."

"Good night." The words came out in a near whisper.

"Sweet dreams." He gave her his sexy smile that melted her before he turned away and walked down the steps.

She watched him go, not wanting him to leave. But she'd see him in the morning—she had that to look forward to.

At her gate, he looked back. "Go on in now so that I know you're safely behind your locked door."

She smiled. "This is King Creek."

"I'm not leaving until you do it." His voice sounded teasing, but she knew he meant it.

She opened the squeaky screen door, then unlocked and opened her front door, pausing to wave before she walked in and shut it behind her.

For a moment, she stood and listened, hearing the gate squeak then close behind him.

It had been an exhilarating day. She couldn't wait for tomorrow and spending a lot more time with CJ.

4

unday morning dawned bright and cheerful. Yesterday's time with CJ had been so much fun that Jillian woke up smiling the next morning. She'd been disappointed that he hadn't kissed her when he dropped her off, but she appreciated that he was taking things slow with her.

She paced the living room feeling jittery and impatient, even though CJ still had another couple of minutes to arrive on time.

Not one minute later, he pulled up in his shiny yellow Dodge Ram and climbed out. Jillian nearly bounced on her toes with excitement. She might as well have been a teenager, the way she felt at seeing the tall, sexy cowboy striding up the walkway.

The sound of his boots on the steps leading up to the porch rang out in time with the beats of her heart. The doorbell chimed, and she had to force herself to walk slowly to grab her purse off an end table and her jean jacket from the back of the recliner.

She reached the front door, took a deep breath, and gripped the knob a moment before opening it.

There he stood on the other side of the screen, looking mouthwatering tall and heart-stopping sexy.

"Good morning, CJ." The screen door squeaked as she pushed it open and smiled up at him.

"Hi, Jillian." He returned her smile. "Ready?"

"Most definitely." She tugged her jacket on over her fuchsia button-up blouse and fell into step with him as they trotted down the stairs and headed along the walkway. The cool air brushed her cheeks, but the bright morning sun promised to warm the day as it crept up the sky. "It's gorgeous out."

He flashed her a grin. "Not nearly as gorgeous as the woman I'm with."

Her cheeks heated, and she tried to keep her voice steady. "Keep that up, and it will go to my head."

He chuckled. "Sayin' it like I see it."

Jillian's mom had taught her to accept compliments graciously, even if she disagreed, which had everything to do with her lack of self-confidence. So, she simply said, "Thank you."

CJ helped her into the passenger seat, jogged to the driver's side, and climbed into the cab. In moments, they were well on their way to Carter's ranch.

"Been a good long while since I've seen your brothers." CJ looked like he was thinking it over as he guided the truck onto the road leading out of her neighborhood. "I saw them a couple of times early on in my military career, but over the years, it seemed that as soon as I got home to visit my mom and dad, it was time to go back to wherever I was stationed at the time."

"You probably haven't met Kit or the twins." She grinned at the thought of the girls. "Everyone fell in love with Kit the moment we ate the dinner she'd made for Carter's birthday. She'd just started as his new cook, which was crazy since she'd been an L.A. chef at a ritzy restaurant before coming out to his ranch."

CJ looked impressed. "How old are his kids?"

Jillian scrunched her eyebrows. "I think Olivia and Emily are almost eight." She shook her head. "I remember the day they adopted the girls. They were so precious." She smiled at the memory. "Kit has an older son, Noah, who's not much younger than Haylee. He visits every now and then from San Francisco and is a good guy, and has his own family now. He loves the twins to pieces, like the rest of us."

CJ came to a stop sign and waited for a car to pass before pulling onto the road leading out of King Creek. "I hope to get a chance to meet Carter's family."

"I'm sure you will, sooner or later, if not today." Jillian looked out the window at the mesquite trees starting to bud after a long winter. She turned back to CJ. "Do you have any extended family?"

He shrugged. "Aunts, uncles, and cousins here and there. I'm closest to my cousin John, but he lives in Florida, so I don't see him often enough."

Out of curiosity, she thought about asking CJ if he wanted kids someday, but she didn't want him to get the wrong idea that she might be thinking of him as husband material. Maybe he was the marrying kind, but it was too soon to have those thoughts in her head.

It was less than twenty minutes to Carter's place from Jillian and Leeann's home, so it wasn't long before they reached the dirt road leading to Superstition Springs Ranch. It was well-graded, so it was an easy mile to the front gate. A Border Collie trotted out to greet the newcomers, barking to alert everyone that someone had arrived.

They drove up to the rustic, sprawling home surrounded by a bunkhouse, a small cottage in the back, corrals, sheds, and a big red barn. Carter also had multiple fields, corrals, and a whole lot of acreage.

CJ whistled as he took in their surroundings. "Carter has a hell of an operation here."

"It's the biggest ranch in the valley." Jillian felt a sense of pride for her brother's success. "Even bigger than our family ranch."

They climbed out of the truck, and the Border Collie stopped barking when she spotted Jillian. She wagged her tail madly as she loped over to Jillian who crouched down and hugged the dog.

"CJ, meet Lucy." Jillian looked up at him as she stroked the dog's head. "She's been with Carter since she was a puppy, which has been a while." She hugged the dog again. "You're the best cattle dog ever."

She stood and spotted Carter coming around the corner. She waved, and Carter grinned as he strode their way.

"Hey, sis," he said as he reached them. He held out his hand to CJ. "Damned good to see you."

CJ gripped Carter's hand for a moment. "We'll have to go out to Mickey's and get caught up soon."

"Deal." He nodded toward the road. "Kit and the girls should be home soon. I'd love to have you meet them."

"That would be my pleasure." CJ smiled. "Jillian tells me your daughters are eight now and that your wife is one hell of a cook."

"True on both accounts." Carter tipped his head in the direction of the big red barn. "I'll introduce you to Faith."

"Been looking forward to it." CJ joined Carter and they headed toward the barn. CJ looked over his shoulder, waiting for her to catch up, but she motioned him to go on with her brother. He and Carter had things to talk about and Jillian didn't mind walking behind them.

. . .

CJ DIDN'T WANT Jillian to feel left out, but she looked content to follow. He listened to Carter as he talked about the young mare.

"Faith has really come along." Carter gestured toward a corral where a couple of horses ate alfalfa. "She's sharp as a tack and then some."

They reached the corral. CJ stood on ground and rested his forearms on the top rail as he studied the chestnut-colored appaloosa with a white mottled rump and a leopard appaloosa.

Carter nodded toward the beautiful leopard appaloosa. "Faith is two years old and knows her way around a ranch. That girl's got a lot of spirit."

CJ looked at his old friend. "Mind if I give the girls a couple of treats?"

"Not at all." Carter stepped back from the railings. "Tell you what. I'll take Cassie into the barn, and you can spend some time with Faith."

Carter opened the gate and caught the chestnut appaloosa by her bridle. CJ followed and went up to Faith as Carter walked away with Cassie.

Faith greeted him with a snort. "Well, hello, girl." CJ fished his hand in his pocket. He brought out a peppermint and held it out on his palm. Faith snuffled his hand, her soft muzzle brushing his skin. She took the peppermint, then bobbed her head up and down.

CJ grasped her bridal and stroked her forehead. "You are a beautiful young lady." Faith had a white base coat with brown spots all over her hide and striped hooves, an appaloosa characteristic trait. He'd always loved leopard appaloosas.

Faith snuffled his jacket, looking for more treats. He dug out another peppermint, and she took it from his palm. He ran his hand over her shoulder and forearm, feeling the solid muscle.

"She's gorgeous," Jillian said, catching his attention.

CJ looked from Faith to where Jillian stood on the second rail, and he smiled. Faith wasn't the only gorgeous female here.

"She sure is." CJ raised his head and nodded to Carter as he approached. "How much do you want for this sweetheart?"

Carter stood on the other side of Faith's head and named a more than reasonable figure.

"I'll take her." CJ released Faith's bridle. "I mentioned on the phone about that foreman selling off all the ranch assets. I'm now in the market for a horse trailer, among other things. "Got one you're willing to part with?"

Carter shook his head. "I tell you what, there's going to be an auction next weekend at the rodeo grounds, where you're likely to find at least some of the things you need." He cocked his head toward the back of the barn. "In the meantime, I'd be happy to haul this girl out to your place tomorrow if you'll be home."

"Thank you." CJ nodded. "It'll give me time to run into King Creek to get some alfalfa and wet COB." Most horses seemed to like the mixture of corn, oats, and barley with molasses.

"Good deal." Carter moved toward the gate. "I'll get her to your ranch before noon."

CJ patted Faith's neck. "See you tomorrow, beautiful lady."

The mare snorted, bobbed her head, and knocked off CJ's Stetson. Jillian laughed as CJ scooped it up and slapped it against his thigh before settling it on his head again.

Carter closed the gate behind them and Lucy plopped her butt down in the dirt at his side. "I've got a pitcher of iced tea in the fridge if you'd like to join me."

"Wish I could." CJ looked at the sky before meeting Carter's gaze. "I have a date with some Australian shepherds."

"Bear gave you some names, I take it," Carter said as they walked toward CJ's truck.

CJ nodded. "Figured I'd check out the Aussies, first. I've always had a soft spot for them."

They shook hands again, and Carter slapped CJ on the shoulder. "Give me a call, and we'll meet up at Mickey's sometime soon."

CJ grinned. "You've got it." He helped Jillian into the passenger seat before heading to the driver's side.

Carter stopped him, a serious look on his features. "Take care of my little sister."

"Count on it," CJ said with a smile before opening the door and climbing behind the wheel.

He stuffed the key into the ignition and turned, and the engine came to life. He looked at Jillian. "Ready to see some puppies?"

She gave an enthusiastic nod. "Can't wait."

They waved at Carter before taking off down the dirt road back to the highway.

So far, the morning had been perfect. He was spending time with a beautiful woman and he'd found a horse that was the perfect fit.

Now for a puppy.

The breeder was on the other side of King Creek. He had a good time talking with Jillian on the ride there. She was fun with a great personality, and she was sexy as hell.

Carter's warning wasn't unexpected—the McLeod boys had always been protective of their little sisters. But it did give him pause. Once he had his ranch back up and running, he planned to sell it and travel, provided the offer he'd been given came through. If things went farther with him and Jillian, would she want to leave King Creek to travel with him?

Too soon to start thinking about that. Maybe he should tell her now of his plans? But he didn't even know if he would sell the ranch for sure, so he'd take it a day at a time with her. As soon as he knew more, he could talk with her about it—if they were still seeing each other.

If he had anything to do with it, they would be. He liked what he saw in her a whole lot.

Didn't take long to get to the Anderson's place. They parked in front of the home that was on a small piece of property. A few head of cattle grazed on the other side of a fence, the field near the weathered barn.

Two Australian shepherds trotted up to them, barking. It looked more like they were greeting them, but they'd no doubt be as protective as hell if need be.

CJ stepped out and greeted the dogs, but they stood back and barked. They weren't being aggressive, just doing their job, alerting their master.

A man opened the door and hobbled out while instructing the dogs to quiet down. CJ shook the old man's hand. "I'm CJ Jameson."

Before he could help Jillian out of the truck, she had climbed out and joined them. The breeze picked up, blowing strands of hair across her face and the scent of her honeysuckle perfume straight to him.

She brushed the hair away and held out her hand. "Hi. I'm Jillian McLeod."

"A hell of a lot of McLeods around these parts." The old man took her hand. He released it and nodded in the direction of the yard. "The puppies are in the back."

He shuffled to the gate and let them through before shutting it. They followed him to the fenced-in backyard, where four puppies played in a pen on the grass near an oak bench. The yard was well-kept, the water in the pen was sparkling clean, and the puppies looked happy and healthy.

"I only have one male and two female breeders and have one litter each a year." The man reached the pen and smiled at the puppies, who ran up to the barrier and greeted him. He rubbed their heads. "I don't run a damned puppy mill like some no-good SOBs."

Jillian knelt beside the fence, reached in, and let the little ones sniff and lick her hand. "They're so cute."

The man opened the gate and let in CJ and Jillian. "Usually let them run around the yard, but it's easier to meet them when I put them in the pen."

Jillian sat cross-legged in the grass and was immediately tackled by squirming and licking puppies. She giggled as one of them crawled into her lap and licked her nose. It was black and white with patches of red on its face and had one blue eye and one brown.

CJ crouched next to her and chuckled as the other three greeted him with enthusiasm.

"They're twelve weeks old, and I've been working on the basics with them." Mr.

Anderson sat on the bench near the pen. "I start out training them early with a whistle, and I recommend continuing with that method when you take your puppy home."

"We had Aussies when I was growing up, and we used a whistle for commands." CJ smiled at the fond memories that came to mind. "I'll need a refresher."

"I can recommend a good trainer if you need extra help. I don't know much about computers, but Bear tells me you could find good resources there," the old man said. "Are you looking for one or two?"

"My operation won't be very big, at least not at the beginning." CJ stroked the head of the puppy in Jillian's lap. "One is enough to start with."

"Every ranch needs a good dog." Jillian grinned at CJ, which caused a low burn in his belly. Damn, but he loved her smile.

They spent some time with the puppies. All had one blue

eye and one brown, a couple with more red patches than the other two.

The one CJ liked best was the same one that hung around Jillian the most.

He looked at Anderson. "Did you name them?"

The old man nodded. "It's important to start their training. You can keep the name or give them a new one." He pointed to the one Jillian held in her lap. "That there's Sadie." He gestured to each of the others. "Billy, Sally, and Sophie."

"I'll take Sadie." CJ took the puppy in his arms and stood, then held out one hand to Jillian to help her to her feet.

"She's so perfect." Jillian smiled and bounced on her toes, looking as excited as he felt.

They followed Anderson into his kitchen, which smelled of roast beef and potatoes cooking in a crockpot on a counter.

He led them to a dining table, and they took seats while he went to get some paperwork.

Jillian held onto the puppy that squirmed in her arms, and she giggled as it licked her face. "You are such a beautiful girl." She shifted Sadie in her lap.

He returned with Sadie's AKC registration, microchip information, as well as vet and shot records. He included a bag of the premium dog food he'd raised the puppies on and instructed them on when to worm the puppy.

CJ had brought his checkbook in case the breeder didn't take credit cards, so he wrote a check for the amount Anderson had given him.

"Get her spayed at six months," Anderson said. "Call me if you have any questions."

"Will do." CJ got to his feet just as the old man did, and Jillian rose with the puppy. She looked so sweet, hugging the little critter. CJ reached out a hand to Anderson. "Thank you much."

The man showed them to the door, and they headed out to the truck. CJ took the puppy in his arms and helped Jillian into the truck. She put on her seatbelt before taking the wiggly Aussie from him and squeezing her close.

She shifted Sadie in her lap as she looked at CJ. "Do you have everything she'll need?"

He shook his head. "I need to run to Hannigan's Feed Store and get what I don't have. I'll need a portable crate to put her in when I transport her. She'll be safer in a vehicle that way. She'll also need a collar and leash, and I'll get her tag while I'm there."

"I can go with you and hang onto Sadie if you'd like."

He glanced from the road to her and smiled. "I'd much appreciate that."

He turned his attention back to the road as they chatted and drove into town.

Soon after they arrived at Hannigan's, they strode inside, and Bill Taylor greeted them. He'd heard the man's son had gone to prison a year or so ago, and the haggard look on the man's face might have had something to do with it. He'd moved to town long after CJ left for the military, so he'd never met the man's son.

Bill was friendly and helpful, and it wasn't long before CJ was loaded with feed for the horse, everything the puppy would need, and then some. While they shopped, the puppy had wanted down so that she could explore, but Jill held on to her. He could just imagine how she and Sadie could be in his life forever, just the three of them.

He put the Aussie in the crate, secured it on the back seat, and then drove Jillian home.

By the time they reached her place, it was almost five. They said goodbye at the front gate so that Sadie wouldn't be left alone in the truck.

CJ brushed a loose strand of hair from her cheek, and she

shivered. "Thank you for going with me today to see the horse and the puppies. I enjoyed having you with me."

"I had a good time." She moved her gaze to the truck and back to him. "You'll have a couple of great new friends in Faith and Sadie."

"I think you're right." He stared into her beautiful eyes, wanting to kiss her so damn bad he ached with it. But he was taking it slow with her.

She looked like she wanted him to kiss her, too, and it was all he could do to keep his hands off her and step back. She hesitated before saying," Goodbye," then headed for the house.

CJ watched Jillian until she stood on the porch, unlocking the door. She turned and looked at him like she didn't want their day to end. She smiled and waved, disappearing into the house and closing the door behind her.

Several heartbeats later, he climbed into his truck and headed home with Sadie.

5

Butterflies tumbled through Jillian's belly as she rushed around her flower shop with last-minute preparations for her grand opening. In moments, she would be an official florist. Her brother, Bear, had draped a *Grand Opening* sign across the top of the store's front wall, and the window displays looked beautiful.

The room smelled of fresh paint but also of flowers and greenery.

"Are you ready?" Leeann walked out of the back room and looked at her phone. "You have one minute to put on your business face."

"What if no one comes in?" Jillian looked at the front door, wringing her hands, wishing a line of customers were ready to enter.

"Take a deep breath and smile." Leeann strode to the entrance and removed the key that had been dangling from a holder on her wrist. She unlocked the door, then turned and beamed at Jillian. "It's official. You're now a businesswoman." She batted at the bells hanging from the door, and they jangled cheerfully.

Haylee peeked in through the backroom doorway. "Is someone here?"

"That's just Leeann." Jillian pulled her phone out of her pocket and checked the time. "Kara's late, and there are no text messages from her." Jillian walked around the counter. She brushed her palms down her navy-blue slacks, then adjusted her scoop-neck blouse, feeling jittery and on edge. "She's been on time every day this week to help get the shop ready for our grand opening. Hopefully, she's all right."

"Calm down. I'm sure she's just running behind schedule." Leeann rested her hand on Jillian's forearm. "Take a deep breath, sis, like I told you to."

Jillian inhaled, filling her lungs before she slowly let it out. She shook out her arms, trying to get rid of some of the tension that had gripped her all morning.

"Now, smile." Leeann gave her an encouraging look.

Jillian smiled, but her nerves wouldn't let her relax. She peered through the doorway leading to the backroom. "The baskets look great, Haylee."

"Thanks." Her sister's long, blonde braid swung over her shoulder as she focused on one of her creations for the front displays. "This is fun for me."

The bells jangled. Jillian startled and turned to see CJ striding through the doorway, holding Sadie's leash as the puppy trotted at his side.

Warmth flushed through her at the sight of the tall, sexy cowboy. His cute grin had her smiling back at him as tingles raced through her from head to toe.

He reached the counter, and she wished it wasn't between them. If it hadn't been, she might have thrown her arms around him, so maybe it was better the barrier was there.

"It all looks great." He let his gaze move around the shop,

taking in the sparkling new cases and displays. "You've done a terrific job."

"With a lot of help." Jillian squeezed her hand into a fist on the countertop, tension gripping her again. "The rose order is running late. This morning, they called to let me know that law enforcement closed down I-10 for a major accident at the tunnel."

"They'll be here soon." CJ put his hand over hers, lending her strength. "Let me know if there's anything I can do to help."

Jillian's phone rang, and she slid her hand from beneath his. She raised her finger. "Just a sec." She tugged her phone out of her pocket and saw Kara's name on the screen. She accepted the call and brought the phone to her ear. "Is everything okay, Kara?"

"I'm so sorry, Jillian." The young woman's voice came out in a snuffly croak. "I've got a cold."

Jillian's stomach bottomed out. She felt bad for the teenager, but it left her without a delivery person.

"I hope you feel better soon." Jillian gripped her phone so tightly her fingers ached.

"Thank you." Kara had a coughing fit. When she stopped, she said, "It's grand opening day. I should be there."

"Just rest and take care of yourself." Jillian tried to put a smile into her voice. "We'll see you when you're over your cold."

When Jillian disconnected the call, panic overwhelmed her. "What am I going to do without a delivery person?"

"I'll happily be at your service today." CJ scooped up the puppy. "I have Sadie's crate, and I just picked up a small fence. Can she hang out in your backroom? Puppies sleep most of the time, anyway."

"Of course she can." Jillian met CJ's gaze. "Are you sure you want to do my deliveries?"

"Yep." He flashed her a grin. "I just need to get everything out of my truck. I'll grab a bag of puppy food from Hannigan's first and be right back.

Leeann took Sadie out of his arms and hugged her. "Ooooh, we get to watch this precious girl."

CJ strode toward the entrance, and Jillian watched the way his Wranglers hugged his tight ass, and she sighed.

Leeann stood beside her. "Yep. He's got one sexy ass."

Jillian shot a look at her sister, who smirked back at her.

The landline rang, grabbing Jillian's attention. She snatched the receiver off its cradle. "It's a beautiful day at Desert Blooms. How may I help you?"

"I'd like to send an arrangement to a sick friend at King Creek Hospital," a croaky female voice said. "Can you deliver it today?"

"Yes, ma'am." Jillian's heart buoyed. "We'll make the perfect arrangement for you."

The woman told Jillian what she wanted then gave her information, including her credit card. Jillian entered everything into an app on the iPad she had on the counter.

She hung up the phone as Leeann's excited voice came from the back. "An online order just came in for a chocolate-lovers gift basket."

"Wonderful." Jillian peered through the doorway and saw Leeann with the puppy in one arm and an iPad in her opposite hand. Jillian smiled at the sight. "We had a call for a get-well arrangement, too. She wants sunflowers, chrysanthemums, and daisies."

Her cell phone rang. She didn't recognize the number, but she wanted to answer all calls to make sure she didn't miss anything important.

It was the delivery truck driver, telling her the accident had cleared and they'd arrive within the hour.

She held her hand to her chest and breathed a sigh of relief. "The roses are back on their way."

"Yay!" Leeann, who was still holding the Aussie, cheered and waggled the puppy's paw. "Sadie's excited, too."

"Awesome." Haylee raised a gift basket. "And another ready for your display."

"You're both the best." Jillian beamed at them.

Bells jangled. Jillian figured CJ had returned, so when she turned, she was surprised to see a gentleman in his forties walking up to the refrigerated cases.

"Welcome to Desert Blooms," she said, and the man turned to face her. "Can I help you find something?"

His brow furrowed. "I don't see any roses."

"Our delivery will be here soon." Jillian rounded the counter and walked up to him. "Are you looking for long-stemmed?"

He nodded. "My wife loves orange roses." His expression turned hopeful. "Will you have any?"

She smiled. "Yes, and they're grown right here in Maricopa County."

"Great." The man smiled back at her. "Our anniversary is today, so I'd like to pick them up when I get off work, around 5:30. How late are you open?"

"Until 6:00 p.m." She picked up the iPad. "Let me take your information, and I'll have the bouquet ready for you when you come by." She gestured to a display stand. "Would you like to purchase a vase for them?"

Jillian started inputting the order as the man perused the crystal and porcelain vases. He chose a green glass vase that would look beautiful with the orange roses. He went to the card rack and chose an anniversary card. After she got his contact information and he paid, the man left with a spring in his step, the card in his jacket pocket.

CJ arrived not long after, carrying a crate and a bag of dog food. Jillian stepped aside so that he could take the crate to the back room. He went out again, returned with the fence, a few toys, and bowls for water and food, and set it all up in a corner. He put the crate inside the fence with the door open.

Leeann didn't want to put the puppy down, but she did as the iPad chimed, signaling another order, this one for a floral arrangement to be delivered to the accounting firm Jillian used to work for.

The roses arrived, and CJ helped Jillian put them in the display case. She took a dozen of the orange long-stemmed roses into the back along with the green vase.

Haylee put together the arrangements for the accounting office and the hospital. CJ took off with both deliveries then Haylee made a beautiful ombre orange bow for the orange roses.

The morning continued with a steady stream of business. Jillian felt so pumped like her blood was on fire. She barely had time to finish a task before something else called for her attention.

"So far, so good," Jillian said to herself after a woman left with a gift basket.

"Yep." Leeann rested her hand on Jillian's shoulder. "King Creek, watch out for Jillian McLeod."

Jillian smiled at her sister as her phone rang. She looked at it and saw *Grandpa Daniel* on the screen.

She connected the call and brought the phone to her ear. "Hi, Grandpa."

"How's your opening day going, pumpkin?" His voice sounded strong, belying his 98 years.

His endearment always made her smile. "It's going wonderfully." As they spoke, Jillian went up to the greeting card display stand and straightened the cards, ensuring the appropriate envelopes followed their corresponding cards. Only a couple of cards had been purchased so far, so it wasn't any real effort. "We've been busy since opening, and it hasn't let up."

"THAT'S MY GIRL." He coughed, and the sound tugged at her heart.

"Are you okay, Grandpa?" She frowned. "That cough doesn't sound good."

"I'm fine, young lady." His voice strengthened. "I'll stop in and see you later in the week when you might not be so busy."

The thought of her grandpa driving at his age always caused a sense of unease in her, but he was a stubborn, strong, proud man who was determined not to rely on others.

"Your grandma would have been just as proud of you as I am," he went on. "I always knew you were destined for great things."

"Thank you." She gripped her phone tighter as she moved behind the counter. "Your support has meant everything to me."

Bells jangled, and she looked up to see a young woman with a toddler in tow heading straight for the counter.

"Another client just walked in," Jillian said into the phone. "I'd better get back to work."

"I won't keep you," Grandpa said. "Just remember that one of the secrets to being happy in life is to enjoy your job, too."

"Thank you, Grandpa. Talk soon." Jillian disconnected the call, pocketed the phone, and turned her attention to her customer.

CJ PULLED his truck into the parking lot of King Creek Elementary, where he was delivering an arrangement of pink, yellow, and purple tulips. He carried the bouquet into the front office and greeted Mrs. Olson, the secretary, who had been working there since he was in school. The years had been kind to her, and she now was an attractive silver-haired woman in her sixties.

"Well, good morning to you, CJ." The woman smiled, looking up at him from behind a counter. "It's been a very long time—you're all grown up."

CJ grinned as he set the delivery on the countertop. "And you haven't changed a bit."

"That statement makes you my favorite former student." Mrs. Olson laughed and looked at the bouquet. "What beautiful tulips. Who are they for?"

He looked at the card. "Mindy Ross."

"I think this is her planning period." Mrs. Olson picked up her phone, and after speaking to someone and ending the call, she returned her attention to CJ. "She'll be right in."

A few moments later, a stunning blonde walked into the office. Her eyes widened when she saw him. "CJ?"

He stared at his old girlfriend in surprise. "I had no idea you're the same Mindy." He smiled at the leggy woman who had once upon a time stolen his heart. "It's damn—darn—good to see you."

"I got married and then divorced. I just haven't changed it back yet." She gave CJ a hug. "It's good to see you." She felt, looked, and smelled as good as he remembered.

Mindy parted from him. "How are you doing?"

He smiled. "Just moved back to King Creek, and I'm taking over my mom's ranch."

"That's wonderful." She gave a radiant smile. "Welcome home. We'll have to get together sometime and catch up."

"Sounds good." He picked up the arrangement from the countertop. "I'm helping Jillian McLeod at Desert Blooms with her deliveries for today since her normal gal called in sick. These are for you."

"I heard she was opening a flower shop." Mindy took the bouquet from him. "These tulips are gorgeous—they're my favorite." She set them back on the countertop, read the card, and sighed. "They're from my ex."

"Would you like me to put them in the circular file?" Mrs. Olson asked.

Mindy looked at the bouquet. "Seems a shame to toss them." She turned her attention back to CJ. "Thank you for the delivery. It was good to see you, and I hope we can get together soon."

He touched the brim of his hat. "My pleasure."

"Just a sec." She turned to the secretary. "Mrs. Olson, may I have pen and paper?"

"Of course, dear." The woman handed both to Mindy.

Mindy scribbled something on the small notepad, tore off the top sheet, and handed it to CJ. "That's my cell number. Give me a call, and we'll set up a date and time."

He took the paper and saw that Mindy had put a heart next to her name. He folded the sheet and stuck it in his wallet. "Nice to have run into you." He gave a nod to her and then to Mrs. Olson. "I hope you ladies have a great rest of your day."

The two women said goodbye, and he left the shop, thinking about his meeting with his old girlfriend.

Mindy and Jillian were both beautiful, but they couldn't be more different. In high school, he really cared for Mindy, and she'd broken his heart when she ended their relationship. He didn't hold that against her, but he wouldn't call her—not when he was seeing Jillian.

As lovely as Mindy was, as far as he was concerned, she didn't hold a candle to Jillian. But it was far more than beauty— Jillian touched him in a way that he couldn't explain. She was sweet, level-headed, and intelligent. He couldn't remember when he'd had a better time than he'd had with her since the day they'd met.

CJ drove back to the flower shop, parked, and headed inside. Jillian stood by the gift basket display with a woman he knew from his mother's church. Jillian spoke animatedly and wore her beautiful smile.

He wanted to pause and drink her in and enjoy the way her slacks hugged her shapely hips and the curves of her breasts that pressed against her blouse. It was modest but just low enough to show a little cleavage.

His palms itched to touch her, and he wished he had her all to himself. He headed to the back, where Haylee worked on a display, Leeann studied the screen of an iPad, and Sadie slept in her crate.

Haylee looked over the top of a bouquet. "How are the deliveries going?"

"Smooth as glass." He glanced at the puppy pen. "How was Sadie?"

"Perfect little angel." Leeann smiled. "She loves that Lambchop stuffed toy."

CJ grinned. "So far, it's her favorite."

"We have one order ready to go." Leeann inclined her head in Haylee's direction. "We'll have another for you to deliver as soon as Haylee finishes it."

Jillian slipped into the room. "A cookie gift basket just flew off the shelf. The Grand Opening sign is bringing in quite a bit of business."

"I bet it's making people curious," Leeann said. "When they see all you have to offer, they're sold."

Jillian pushed her hair behind her ears. "It already feels like it's been a long day, but I'm so pumped I'm not tired."

"You will be." Haylee laughed. "By the end of the day, you'll be dead on your feet."

"You're probably right." The front doorbells jangled, and Jillian spun to head back in that direction.

CJ couldn't help but watch her walk out of the back room. She had the sexiest ass, and he loved her figure. He had to admire her composure under fire. She'd been going like a mini hurricane all day and handled it well.

He turned back to Leeann and Haylee, and they grinned at him like they knew where his thoughts had been. His interest in Jillian was no doubt easy to read.

CJ waited for Haylee to finish the orders while talking with her and Leeann. When both bouquets were ready to go, he headed out the front with them. He winked at Jillian, who was with one of the ladies who worked as a bank teller down the street. Pink touched Jillian's cheeks, and she gave him a quick smile before focusing on the woman.

He put both orders on the floorboard in the back, then climbed in and drove first toward a church on the north side of town. He passed the fairgrounds where some of the Spring Fling activities would take place. Just past that, a junior competition would be held at the rodeo grounds.

When he reached the church, CJ entered the quiet recesses and was met by a man of the cloth a few steps in. The preacher was pleased with the display, which he set on the altar. Haylee had outdone herself with the arrangement made of Easter lilies, carnations, daisies, and hydrangeas. CJ's mom had loved flowers, and he had a passable knowledge of various types.

After that delivery, CJ headed to a residential address but had to stop behind traffic backed up to the highway leading to the southern end of King Creek.

He leaned out the window and saw that he was five cars behind an accident between a tractor and a truck with a plumber's logo. The truck had taken the worst of the impact, its side smashed in. It didn't look serious, but two men stood between the vehicle and the tractor, yelling at each other, faces purple with fury. They looked close to throwing punches. CJ recognized one of the pair, Wade Milton, who owned the farm on the other side of the nearby fence. CJ didn't know the other man.

He pulled his truck off the highway, climbed out, and strode toward the two men. When he reached them, he said, "Howdy."

Wade and the other man abruptly stopped at the interruption and looked at CJ.

"Nice afternoon, boys. Good to see you, Wade." CJ gave a nod before turning to the other man and holding out his hand. "I haven't had the pleasure. I'm CJ Jameson."

The man hesitated but took CJ's hand and mumbled. "Dave Ross."

Was this man Mindy's ex-husband? If he had as bad a temper as he looked, it might have been a reason they divorced.

When they released grips, CJ looked from Dave to Wade. "What's the problem?"

Wade snarled. "This idiot tried to drive around me without giving me a chance to move to the roadside."

"He wasn't doing no such thing." Dave's face purpled again. "When I tried to pass him, he rammed my truck."

Wade narrowed his gaze. "Since when is passing on the right shoulder legal or smart?"

CJ pushed up his hat and studied the vehicles. Wade was correct, as far as CJ could tell. Dave's truck would have had to pass the tractor on his right since the damage was on the truck's left.

"Tell you what." CJ inclined his head to the road's shoulder. Why don't you both pull over to the side and let traffic pass? I'm sure the sheriff's department can help you sort things out when they get here."

"I have an appointment." Dave gestured to his truck. "Look what he's done—can't drive my truck with that damage."

Wade growled. "Wouldn't have happened if you'd waited to pass me on the left."

Both men balled their fists and glared.

"Go on and move your vehicles out of the way." CJ kept his tone calm. "You're not solving anything by blocking traffic."

Wade spit on the ground before striding to his tractor. The engine growled as he put it into gear and pulled onto the side of the road.

Ross followed. His truck was already mostly on the shoulder and barely looked drivable, but the man managed to get it to limp further to the right.

Sirens sounded in the distance as the backed-up cars began moving past the tractor and truck.

By the time two sheriff's department SUVs arrived, the stopped-up traffic had passed.

The lawmen split the three of them up. CJ explained his part to one of the deputies and told him that he hadn't witnessed the accident, that he'd just been trying to keep the peace between the two.

The deputy let him go, and CJ climbed into his vehicle. He checked the time and saw that he would be late with the delivery if he didn't get going. He drove around the accident scene and headed toward his next destination.

He reached the home, where he handed the bouquet of long-stemmed red roses with baby's breath and greenery to a middle-aged woman who looked surprised and overwhelmed. "I've had such a rough day." Her voice caught, and she held the roses closer to her. "This—this was such a sweet thing for my boyfriend to do."

"I hope the rest of your day is much better." CJ touched the brim of his hat and returned to his vehicle. She had retreated into her home and closed the door behind her by the time he hoisted himself into his truck.

He had a new appreciation for florists. Flowers brought brightness into people's lives, lifting their spirits, even if just for a moment.

When he arrived back at the flower shop, it was closing time, and Jillian locked the door after he walked in.

She turned to him. "Thank you so much for what you did for me today." She rose on her toes and kissed his cheek before stepping back, her face pink. "I couldn't have done it without you and my sisters."

"It was my pleasure, Jillian." He rested his hands on her shoulders. "I'll be happy to help you tomorrow, too."

"Thank you, but I don't want to keep you from your ranch another day." She smiled. "Bear's wife, Rae, is doing the deliveries. They have their three-and-a-half-year-old son in preschool three days a week now, and she said she's been looking for something to do on the days he's not home."

CJ slid his palms down Jillian's arms. He liked the feel of her beneath his touch. "If you need my help at all this week or any time, give me a call."

"Thank you." She cleared her throat. "Would you like to come over to my and Leeann's home for a celebratory dinner?" She glanced toward the backroom and returned her gaze to him. "Haylee made a big pan of sour cream enchiladas, everyone's favorite. Tyson will be there, too."

"Thanks for the invite, but I'd better get Sadie home." He stepped back. "It's been a long day for that pup."

Jillian looked disappointed, but she inclined her head to the backroom. "She'll be excited to see you. That girl loves her daddy."

"She's found her way into my heart already." He followed

Jillian to the back, where Haylee sat in the pen with Sadie and played tug-of-war with the little one.

Haylee glanced up. "I'm not ready to let her go."

CJ grinned. "I'm not surprised."

With Haylee's help, he gathered the toys, food and water bowls, puppy food, and with the fence, took it all to his truck. When he returned, Jillian carried the Aussie to his vehicle while he loaded the crate. He hefted Sadie into his arms and transferred her to the crate before closing the door behind him.

A streetlight lit Jillian's features as she held her arms around herself. She shivered as the chill wind stirred her dark hair around her shoulders.

She caught her breath as he took her into his embrace and brought her to him. She smelled sweet, like orange blossoms and cool night air. "Let me warm you up," he said.

"You're comfortable." She snuggled against him, and he held her for a long moment. She tipped her head back to meet his gaze. "Thank you again."

"Anytime." He brushed his lips over hers, and another shiver ran through her. He wanted to kiss her fully, but he'd been waiting for the right time. He didn't want to rush things with her.

She stepped back, out of his arms, and smiled. "Have a good night."

"I'll call you tomorrow." He touched his fingers to the brim of his hat. "Good night, Jillian. Now, go inside before you freeze your ass off."

"You don't have to tell me twice." She gave him a little wave and hurried back into the shop.

CJ headed home, his thoughts filled with Jillian. In such a short time, she had such a hold on his heart that he couldn't imagine not having her in his life.

He shook his head. He had a habit of jumping into things feet first, and he just hoped he wasn't headed for heartache.

But then, a relationship wasn't such a good idea when he wasn't sure he'd hang around King Creek forever.

He blew out a long breath as he guided his truck onto the dark highway. He had to get his head on straight and figure things out sooner rather than later. The last thing he wanted to do was break Jillian's heart if he decided he would sell the property and wouldn't be sticking around.

6

Today was Sunday and Jillian's store was closed, and she had an outing with CJ to look forward to. King Creek's week-long Spring Fling festival had started Saturday, and she would be going with him.

The week had sped by, with the flower shop bringing in a good amount of business. Jillian was thrilled with the way everything had gone. There had been some hiccups, but nothing she hadn't been able to work through.

CJ had called every evening once she'd had a chance to wind down from the day. She had a store to run six days a week until she had a good grasp on what it would take to make and keep her business successful and felt comfortable hiring someone to cover when she was out.

Saturday, while she was in the shop, CJ had gone to an auction and purchased things he needed to run his ranch. He'd told her that once he had everything he required in place, he would start buying cattle and getting a couple more horses. She would have liked to have gone with him, but she'd known from the outset the kind of time commitment opening a new store would require.

She was excited for the day as she picked out a navy-blue broomstick skirt, a bright-white blouse, and navy flats. She selected silver earrings to go with the ensemble and a white sweater to ward off the evening chill.

CJ arrived right on time at 1:00 p.m. Leeann had already left to go to the festival with friends. He brushed his lips over Jill's, and she shivered as he helped her into the truck. He still hadn't given her a full-fledged soul-singeing kiss, but even though it seemed a lot longer, they'd only known each other for a week.

At the fairgrounds, they had to park a good distance from the entrance. It seemed like everyone in King Creek had turned out for the festival. The weather was perfect, so she left her sweater behind when he helped her out of the truck.

Hand-in-hand, they strolled through the gate and into the lively crowd. Giggles filled the air as children wove around adults, clutching colorful balloons. A red one bounced against CJ's head. He swiped it away with an amused expression, and Jillian laughed.

They passed food vendors, the breeze carrying mouthwatering smells of Native American fry-bread, corn dogs, and barbeque pork.

"Are you hungry?" CJ led her toward the vendors. "I'm starving."

She grinned. "I could eat a roomful of tacos."

He laughed and escorted her to a taco truck. "Your wish is my command."

They ordered and walked away with sodas and Styrofoam containers filled with rice, beans, and tortillas stuffed with beef barbacoa, along with limes, salsa, and hot sauce on the side. They found places at the picnic benches to sit, where they chatted and enjoyed their lunch.

Finished with their feast, they meandered further into the fairgrounds, their fingers entwined. Jillian said hello to several friends and acquaintances as they made their way. She'd lived her entire life in King Creek, and it felt like she knew almost everyone. In truth, a lot of outsiders had moved to town over the past few years, looking for a quiet place to retire or a small community to raise their kids in.

CJ, on the other hand, only ran into a couple of his old friends. But then, he'd been away for a long time.

A mariachi trio played as six senoritas dressed in red, blue, green, pink, white, and yellow gracefully moved to the music on a temporary stage, their brilliant skirts swirling above their ankles. CJ and Jillian came to a stop in the crowd surrounding the stage and enjoyed the dancing. The young women tap-danced while clicking wooden castanets.

After the number, CJ and Jillian moved on to the artists' vibrantly decorated stalls. They first came to one with displays of beautiful handmade Native American silver jewelry created with turquoise, malachite, coral, and opal.

"I've always loved Native American jewelry." Jillian ran her finger over a silver and turquoise bracelet. "This is gorgeous."

CJ gestured to a man's ring with a large malachite stone. "That looks like a ring my dad had. I don't know what happened to it, but I would have loved to have it." He shook his head. "All my mom's jewelry is gone, too. She had a lot of Native American pieces."

Jillian wondered if the man who had sold off all his property had done the same with his parents' jewelry, but she didn't want to bring it up.

"Oh, this is beautiful." She held a silver and turquoise tear-drop-shaped pendant in her palm. "I'm going to celebrate a successful opening week by splurging on this." She looked up at CJ and smiled. "It's been a long time since I've treated myself."

He matched her smile. "You deserve it."

She paid for the pendant and a chain to go with it. After she threaded the chain through the eye, CJ took the necklace from her and turned her around by her shoulders. She lifted her hair so that he could secure it around her neck, and she turned to face him.

He arranged her hair around her shoulders. "Beautiful."

She held her fingers to the stone at the base of her throat. "Thank you."

He slid his arm around her shoulders. "Let's see what else we can find."

They came up to a chocolatier's stall decorated with hearts and roses, and CJ bought a box of four extra-large chocolate-dipped strawberries. He handed one to Jillian and she enjoyed the taste of the creamy milk chocolate and juicy, sweet strawberry.

"Oh, my God, this is fabulous." She took another bite.

He chewed and swallowed his chocolate strawberry "Damn, these are good. I might end up wishing I bought a dozen."

They came across a stall containing gold-framed paintings and bronze sculptures. "This artist is so talented." She looked at CJ. "Did you know Haylee's an artist? She has another showing going on in Scottsdale."

He shook his head. "I'd love to see her work."

"She began painting full-time after she and Tyson started dating." Jillian slipped her hand into CJ's, and they strolled to the next booth. "Now she handles their nonprofit and paints."

He squeezed Jillian's fingers. "What kind of nonprofit do they have?"

"A horse rescue ranch." She tugged on CJ's hand. "There's my sister-in-law Marlee. She's doing face painting—she does it to raise money for various organizations at just about every event that comes up."

They reached the stall, where Marlee artfully designed flowers on a little girl's face. She painted the finishing touches on her cheek, and the girl's mother slid a folded five into an acrylic moneybox with a sign painted with a 4-leaf clover above "Donate to King Creek 4-H."

Jillian moved to her sister-in-law's side. "Hi, Marlee."

"Jillian." Marlee broke into a broad smile. "How is your grand opening going? Sorry I haven't had a chance to stop by yet."

"My first week went very well." She glanced at CJ then Marlee. "This is CJ Jameson. He used to run around with Colt and Carter when they were in high school, and he recently moved back to King Creek." She turned to CJ. "Meet Marlee, Colt's wife."

"Hello, CJ." Marlee stood and held out her hand. "Welcome home."

He took it in his. "Thank you. I haven't had a chance to give Colt a call since I've been back."

"We'll have to get together soon." She released CJ's hand. "We'd love to have you both over for dinner, and you and Colt can catch up." She smiled at Jillian. "And I can spend time with one of my favorite sisters-in-law."

Jillian laughed. "Considering you have seven of them, you have a lot of favorites."

Marlee grinned. "I love every last one of you."

"Getting together sounds fun." CJ slid his hand around Jillian's. "Colt has my number."

"Great," Marlee said. "And I have Jill's."

CJ touched the brim of his hat. "Have a nice afternoon, Marlee."

"See you." Jillian smiled as she and CJ started to leave the booth.

Marlee gave them a little wave, and they continued on through the stalls.

"Your sister-in-law is nice." CJ smiled down at Jillian. "Colt chose well."

Jillian nodded. "Haylee, Leeann, and I are fortunate sisters because we love all of our brothers' wives." She shook her head. "And we adore all the kids. Their parents breed like rabbits."

CJ chucked. "How many nieces and nephews?"

"Nine counting Carter's stepson, although Noah is more like a brother to Leeann, Haylee, and me since he's close to our ages." She smiled. "All good kids. Their parents raised them well."

"Your mom and dad didn't do a shabby job, either." CJ squeezed her hand. "You all turned out pretty well, too."

"Thanks." She smiled then caught sight of a card reader ahead. "Ooh, let's have our angel tarot cards read."

"What's an angel card?" He let her lead him in the direction of a stall with a beautifully painted cardboard angel with gold wings in front.

"They tend to be more positive and uplifting than traditional tarot cards. At least *I* think so." She brought him to a stop in front of a small white picket fence with a round table and two chairs on the other side of the fence.

She smiled at the card reader, a woman in her fifties with her silver hair in a loose bun. She wore sparkly gold chandelier earrings and a purple caftan with gold embroidery around the neck opening.

"Hello." Jillian gestured to CJ with her free hand. "I'd like to have my cards read."

CJ touched the brim of his hat. "Howdy, ma'am."

"I'm Beth." The woman motioned for Jillian and CJ to come in through the gate. "Have you had your angel cards read in the past?"

"I have." Jillian inclined her head to CJ. "This will be his first experience." She purposefully didn't mention their names. She didn't like to give away any information.

"Very good." Beth held her hand gracefully out to the chairs in front of the table that had a deck in the center. "Please have a seat."

They sat, and Beth took the chair on the other side of the table.

CJ didn't look uncomfortable, just interested in a new experience. Jillian liked that about him.

Beth took the cards from the center and drew them over to her. "Who would like to go first?"

"I will." Jillian leaned forward, excited to get started.

"I'll do a three-card spread for each of you." Beth shuffled the cards. "Think of a question."

For a moment, Jillian considered it. She wanted to know how successful her business would be. She knew the level of success was up to her and her own actions, but things out of her control could interfere.

Jillian met the woman's dark eyes. "Okay, I have my question."

Beth spread the deck in a fan in front of Jillian. "Choose three and lay them in front of you in order. Don't look at them."

The flutter of her belly was a nervous reaction that she hadn't expected. She drew three cards from different parts of the deck and laid them side-by-side.

The card reader set the deck down then touched the first card Jillian had chosen. "This card speaks to the past's influence on the question." She pressed her finger on the middle card. "This one speaks to the present." She touched the last. "This speaks to the future if you don't change your course of action."

Jillian bit the inside of her lip and wondered if she should have wanted to get a card reading after all. What if it was negative? *A little late for that,* she told herself.

Beth flipped over the first card and nodded to herself. "The Dreamer. This excellent card speaks to creativity, positive outcomes, new opportunities, and independence. When you draw this card, you should be open to circumstances like quitting your job and starting a new career or business."

Jaw nearly dropping from the accuracy, it was all Jillian could do to say nothing. From her side vision, she saw CJ look even more interested.

Beth turned over the second card and looked thoughtful. "Ace of Fire." She studied the card for a moment longer before moving her gaze to Jillian. "According to what I'm seeing, you have already taken a leap of faith, and you are on fire, meaning things are going well for you. However," she continued, "there are many ways your circumstances can play out. But this is good, very good."

She picked up the third card and laid it down. "Four of Water." She was quiet for several seconds. She tapped the card with her index finger. "I see you questioning your direction in the future. Don't let yourself get waylaid by doubts. Look around you and see what you have and can continue to accomplish. Take full advantage." She met Jillian's gaze. "Have faith." She paused. "If you have any grief to work through, don't be afraid to lean on others to help you get through it."

"Grieving is in my future?" Jillian frowned, not liking the sound of that at all.

"The possibility is there. You may need to deal with grief but move forward. Don't let it derail you." Beth cocked her head. "Do you have any other questions?"

Jillian considered it for a moment. "I had doubts, but I took the leap, and it's going well, so you're right about all of that. The third card concerns me, the grief most of all. As far as my dream goes, is failure an option?"

The woman studied Jillian for a long moment. "With you, I don't think so. Remember that the third card speaks to future possibilities if no action is taken. If you focus on the positives and what you have already accomplished and are accomplishing, you will continue to be successful."

Beth turned to CJ. "Are you ready to have your cards read?"

He shook his head. "Your card reading for Jillian was interesting, but I'll pass."

Jillian slid her hand into her skirt pocket and pulled out a small wallet. She placed a twenty on the table and got to her feet. "Thank you, Beth."

CJ stood beside her and touched the brim of his hat. "A pleasure, ma'am."

Beth rose and took Jillian's hand. "The heavens are yours." She released it, took CJ's, and held his gaze. "Be cautious with your endeavor. Go with both your gut instinct and your heart."

Jillian looked from the card reader to CJ. What was that all about?

CJ studied Beth for a moment then gave a single nod. "Have a nice time at the festival, ma'am."

Beth bowed from her shoulders and smiled at CJ, then Jillian. "Go with the Angels' grace."

CJ took Jillian's hand, and they walked away from the angel card reader's stall. "What did you think of your reading?"

"It's mostly for fun, but it was interesting how the first two cards applied to me and my business." She considered all that the card reader had said. "If she is the real deal and the card readings were accurate, I wasn't crazy about the Four of Water."

"Doubts and griefs are common with anyone." CJ shrugged. "It's a sure bet that one day you'll experience grief, and likely most people question what they're doing and the direction they're headed. It's human nature."

"You're right." Jillian gave him an impish grin. "What do you say to some friendly competition at ring toss or the basketball hoop game?"

He laughed. "You're on."

7

As she and CJ headed toward the far end of the fairgrounds, Jillian couldn't help but think about the reading. The first two cards were so accurate that it made it difficult *not* to believe. She mentally shook her head. No sense in dwelling on it. She pushed the thoughts to the back of her mind, determined to immerse herself in their time together and continue to thoroughly enjoy herself.

They ate the last two chocolate-covered strawberries on their way to the games. Jillian's was just as delicious as the first one she'd eaten earlier.

A couple of teenagers were playing at the ring toss booth when CJ and Jillian arrived. The boys joked with each other and traded rude remarks.

CJ leaned close to Jillian. "Their language is a little rough. We can move on."

Jillian was tempted to agree, but the young men were moving away. "They're leaving."

He touched the small of her back, and they stepped forward. Stuffed bears, pandas, and puppies of all sizes hung from above and down the sides of the stall.

"Win a stuffed animal for your girl." The carnie manning the stall flipped a rainbow-colored ring in the air. "It's easy to do." The man held out five of them to CJ. "Five dollars is all it takes. Just get three of these on the pegs, each ring on a different peg."

After taking his wallet out of his pocket, CJ pulled a five, handed it to the carnie, and took the rings in return.

Jillian stepped aside and watched him line up the ring, holding it in front of his face. He tossed it underhand, and it hooked itself on one of the five pegs. He aimed another, but this one missed. He made the third toss but missed the fourth.

He glanced at Jillian. "One more chance."

She smiled. "You can do it."

He lined it up and tossed, but it fell short.

"Good try," she said.

"I'll go another round." CJ handed another five to the carnie and accepted the rings. This time he missed the first two but ringed the last three successfully.

"We have a winner!" the carnie shouted and gestured to the smaller stuffed animals. "Pick one for the lady. If you win again, you can trade up."

"All right." Once again, CJ passed cash to the young man and received the rings in exchange. He made the first three tosses, then the fourth and fifth as well.

"That gets you one of the bigger stuffed animals." The carnie gestured to a medium-sized bear. "Try again for the jumbo-size."

With a smile, CJ looked at Jillian. "What do you think? You're taking it home."

"The medium one is big enough." She gestured to a bear. "How about the purple one?"

The carnie unhooked the amethyst-purple bear and handed it to Jillian before turning his attention to a waiting group.

"It's soft." Jillian hugged the bear to her. "I'll name her Pansy."

CJ looked at her with amusement. "Pansy, huh?"

Jillian grinned. "I had a make-believe friend named Pansy when I was in kindergarten."

Shaking his head, CJ chuckled. "Good choice."

They moved to the basketball hoop game. Jillian handed CJ the teddy bear and then made four of five baskets. The points resulting from her throws didn't add up to enough to qualify for a prize.

A breeze caused Jillian to shiver as she turned to CJ. "Justin's daughter, Kaycee, is competing in the youth rodeo this evening at the rodeo grounds. She's almost eighteen, so it's her last year. Would you like to see her barrel race?"

"Sure." He put an arm around her shoulders as they turned to head back in the direction of the entrance to the fairgrounds. "You need your sweater, too."

"I do." She looked up into the darkening sky as they walked. "The day has gone by so quickly."

"Have I ever told you how beautiful you are?" CJ asked.

She shot her gaze to his, surprised at his change in conversation, and felt embarrassment and pleasure at the same time.

His intense eyes held hers for a moment. "Thank you," she managed to get out before tearing her gaze from his, her face burning.

Along the way through the fairgrounds, he bought a cone of baby blue and pink cotton candy, and they shared the sticky confection.

"I feel like the floss is stuck to my lips," she said. "But the festival wouldn't be the same without cotton candy."

He lowered his head and brushed his mouth over hers, catching her off guard. "Yep. Your lips are sweet."

Her face heated again, and her lips tingled.

CJ held Jillian closer to him as they strolled back through the crowd and out the front entrance. Once they reached his truck, he put the teddy bear on the back seat and helped her onto the front passenger seat. He made his way to the other side of the truck and climbed in.

By the time they reached the rodeo grounds on the other side of the fairgrounds, pink, yellow, and orange streaked the western sky on the horizon. The rodeo lights were on, their brilliance clearly illuminating the grounds.

After helping Jillian out of the truck, CJ held her sweater for her to put on, immediately alleviating the spring night air chill.

A bullhorn sounded, and the air filled with cheers and shouts, indicating a rodeo activity had just begun. When they reached the front gate, another blurt of the bullhorn signified the end of the turn.

CJ paid the entrance fee, and Jillian accepted and scanned the program a youth handed her.

"Junior and senior barrel racing along with saddle and bareback bronc riding are tonight." She looked up. "Kaycee is a senior, so her event will come after the junior event ends."

"Been a long time since I've been to a rodeo," CJ said. "Colt and I did team roping in high school then both competed in the steer wrestling and bareback riding events."

"That's right." Jillian cocked her head. "When we met, you said you rodeoed with Colt."

"A helluvalot of good times." CJ smiled as if with fond memories. "We were always trying to outdo each other. Sometimes, Colt would be the champion, and the next time, I would. We had a bit of a reputation back then."

"I'm not surprised." Jillian shook her head. "I've heard a lot of stories about my brothers over the years. We're always learning about some mischievous thing one or the other did."

"Did you or your sisters ever compete?" CJ asked.

"Just Leeann," Jillian said. "She was pretty good at barrel racing."

They walked across the dusty ground until they reached the grandstands brimming with spectators. CJ followed Jillian until about mid-way up the stands, and she scooted over on the metal bench so that he could sit beside her.

The junior barrel racing event was going on. A slim young woman rode her horse tightly around the barrels, her blonde hair flying out from beneath her western hat.

"Kaycee told me they call it 'chasing the cans.'" Jillian looked at CJ. "But you probably knew that."

He shrugged. "I've likely forgotten more than I remember."

"I doubt that." She turned back as the girl and her horse crossed the line. A time was called, and cheers rose in the stands. "I wonder how good that time is for a barrel racer."

"I couldn't tell you," CJ said. "Who knows how many records have been broken since I rodeoed."

They got absorbed in the competition, and Jillian found herself cheering with the crowd. When the junior event was over, the winning time and horse and rider were announced, and the crowd roared. The town mayor presented a championship buckle to the young woman to great applause.

"Kaycee's event is next. She's racing in the number five position." Jillian looked up from the program. "When she was younger, she was thrown from a horse, and she developed a fear of riding. Justin took her to a horse therapist and then ended up marrying the therapist, Miranda. Along with Kaycee, Justin and Miranda have a five-year-old named Jacob, and Karley, who's hit the terrible twos."

CJ smiled. "Do you want children?"

"I think so." Jillian shrugged. "Right now, I can't think past the next week of my grand opening."

He laughed. "Can't say that I blame you."

Jillian almost asked him if he wanted children but stopped

herself. He'd asked her, yet she felt like asking him would be like they were on a dating game. She wasn't sure why.

A young woman brought her horse to a stop behind the starting line, and the announcer gave the name of the horse and rider. They looked poised on the edge, ready to go. The bullhorn sounded, and they shot toward the cans. They made it look easy, weaving their way in and out. Jillian had never been interested in rodeo other than being a spectator on occasion. But she loved watching barrel racing, especially the times she'd seen Kaycee participate.

Horse and rider shot across the finish line, and the bullhorn rang out again. A few moments later, they called the time, and the crowd cheered.

The next three racers were very good, but one pair bumped a barrel, which would penalize the rider's score. The other riders' times were just shy of the first racer.

"There she is." Jillian pointed to Kaycee as she rode her horse toward the starting line.

"Our next racer is Kaycee McLeod, a King Creek High School senior, on Princess," the announcer said.

The bullhorn sounded, and they bolted toward the cans. Watching Kaycee's artistry in the sport was breathtaking as she and Princess raced around the cans effortlessly.

They shot toward the finish line, and the bullhorn rang out. A moment later, time was called, and the crowd cheered even more loudly.

The announcer shouted, "Kaycee McLeod takes the lead," and Jillian stomped and cheered along with a host of others in the grandstands.

Five more racers followed Kaycee, but no one beat her score.

Jillian and CJ shot to their feet, applauding, when she was announced the winner, and the mayor presented her with a championship buckle.

"I'm so excited for her." Jillian sat down again, breathless from cheering so much. "She's the sweetest girl you could ever imagine."

Jillian had fun watching the saddle bronc and bareback events next. She could tell that CJ enjoyed watching the sports that he once participated in. Jillian knew a couple of the young men, one of whom Kaycee had been dating for the last year, Tatum Holbrook. She saw Kaycee avidly watching her boyfriend bareback riding.

Tatum won the bareback championship, and Jillian saw Kaycee jumping up and down and shouting her excitement. After the mayor presented Tatum with a buckle, Kaycee met him outside the gate with a flying hug.

The end of the bareback competition signaled the end of the rodeo for the evening, so CJ guided Jillian through the crowd, out the entrance, and to his truck. After they were both in, he started the vehicle's big engine and headed out of the parking lot, away from the rodeo grounds.

"I had a wonderful day." She looked at CJ as he drove through the darkness, the amber glow of the dashboard lights illuminating his strong features. "Thank you for a great time."

He cut his gaze from the road to her and put his hand over hers on the center console. "You made the day special, Jillian."

Heat radiated from his hand, filtering its way through her. She turned to look at the bit of scenery she could see speeding by, lit by the headlights.

They arrived at her home a short time later and he remembered to grab the teddy bear off the back seat. As he walked her up the sidewalk and steps, she decided that if he wasn't going to kiss her, *she* would take the bull by the horns and kiss him.

At the top of the stairs, he brought her into his arms and studied her features.

Tingles raced through her body. "Would you like to come in?

I didn't see Leeann's car, though, so no chaperone." She tried for a teasing note, but she was afraid her voice sounded a little shaky.

"I wish I could." He brushed loose hair away from her cheek and tucked it behind her ear. "I need to get home to Sadie. We ended up being out later than I expected."

"I understand," she whispered.

He held her gaze and then lowered his head.

Her breath caught at the firmness of his mouth as it met hers. She sighed as he slipped his tongue between her lips, and she tasted his warm male flavor and breathed in his scent. He kissed her sweetly and thoroughly until she grew lightheaded.

When she was afraid her knees would give out on her, he raised his head and smiled down at her. "I've been wanting to do that since I met you."

Her throat worked, her lips still tingling. "I've wanted the same."

He gave her a slow, sexy smile that stole her breath again. "Honey, that was the first of many."

CJ made Jillian feel so hot that she wanted to fan herself. She managed a smile even though she trembled from the kiss. "I like that idea."

"It's a promise." He kissed her again, and she found herself leaning against him for strength.

After another devastatingly sensual kiss, he took a step back. "Get into the house before I throw you over my shoulder and take you home with me."

She laughed. "All right. I'll let you get home to your other woman."

He grinned. "Does that mean *you* are my woman? I like that thought."

Her face burned, and she was glad he couldn't see her clearly because she was probably bright red. "Go on now."

He flashed her another grin, then waited for her to unlock her door and let herself in. "Goodnight," she said through the screen door.

"Goodnight, beautiful." He turned and headed down the steps and cast a look over his shoulder. "Lock that door, or I'm not leaving."

"Okay, okay." She grinned to herself and shut the door firmly so that he could hear the thud. She flipped on the lights and blinked rapidly in the brightness.

The rumble of his truck engine faded as he drove away, and she waited in the living room, hugging the purple bear, until she couldn't hear the motor any longer.

She was in heaven, and she nearly skipped to her room. His kisses had been worth waiting for. They had been everything she could have imagined and then some.

The entire time she got ready for bed, she relived the taste of him, his touch, and his wonderful masculine scent.

She finally climbed into bed but didn't sleep for a long time. When she finally did, it was with a smile on her face and in her heart.

8

S adie bounded up to CJ when he whistled to her from where he stood at the barn door. She planted her butt on the ground at his feet and woofed. Her training had been coming along, and she had lived up to her breed's reputation for being intelligent and quick to learn.

He used a hand signal, and the Aussie fell into step beside him as he strode back to the house.

The past several weeks had sped by so quickly that CJ didn't know what had happened with the time—it was already well into May. He spent Sundays with Jillian, and stopped by her store and took her out to lunch once or twice during the week. Their time together always seemed much too short.

Meanwhile, things had been going well on the ranch. He had fully repaired the fence line around his property and had the barn and corrals ready for cattle. His property had plenty of grass to feed a decent-sized herd.

He'd purchased two saddles and bridles from a local saddle-maker and other gear from Hannigan's for Faith and another horse once he found a second one to purchase. Hannigan's had been a good place to stock up on alfalfa and wet cob for Faith and the future horse. He was visiting a ranch in Casa Grande on Monday to look at a couple of Quarter horses. Hopefully, one of them would be perfect for what he was looking for.

Auctions had been a good place to purchase tools and equipment he needed for the ranch. A livestock auction was coming up tomorrow, Saturday, that looked promising. His parents had always raised Herefords, and he preferred that breed to others, so he hoped to find enough to fill his needs at the auction.

He'd also bought all new furniture and had painted the interior in preparation for the sale. In one of their conversations about the transaction, Jim Butcher had requested that he have the place ready to go inside and out. For several million dollars, CJ had no problem with the request. If he decided not to sell, he still liked the idea of sprucing up the house and replacing kitchen appliances and furniture since everything owned by his mom was decades old.

The only thing he didn't plan on doing was building the bungalows that would eventually be added onto the ranch for more of the entertainment company's future guests.

CJ climbed up the steps to his front door and entered the cool interior. May sunshine poured in through the windows, brightening the place as he walked into his kitchen.

He tried to imagine his home being used as the main house for a dude ranch and was having a hard time doing so. He had grown up here and having a bunch of strangers in the house instead of him just seemed not quite right.

What would his mom and dad think if they were still alive? He had a feeling neither one of them would approve of him selling the property to become a dude ranch. They'd been ranchers their entire lives and hadn't known anything different. But he had, and he wasn't sure he fit the mold anymore.

He did figure neighbors wouldn't be too pleased about the sale, but he couldn't make everyone happy. Jillian was the one person in the world he wanted to make happy, but he wasn't even sure if he could do that.

One day at a time. He'd have to sit down and evaluate his business and life plans and talk with Jillian about them. It wasn't fair to her to continue the relationship if she didn't want to go with him.

CJ opened the new stainless-steel fridge and pulled out a stoneware jug of iced tea. He took a tumbler out of a cabinet, filled it with ice from the freezer, and poured himself a glass.

He leaned against the counter and drank the entire contents before filling the tumbler again.

Sadie sat at his feet, always seeming content to be at his side. She'd been great company since he'd brought her into his home, and he was happy to have her. His future was still uncertain, but he intended to take the Aussie with him wherever he ended up.

He refilled her water and food bowls before making himself a roast beef sandwich and eating it at the kitchen table. The puppy curled up on a bed in a nearby corner of the room.

If it weren't for Sadie, he'd have been lonely—she was good company. He slid his phone from its holster as he ate and checked for emails, finding one from Jim Butcher. He hadn't heard from Jim since their last phone conversation. The man wanted an update on CJ's progress with the ranch and seemed anxious to move forward as soon as the operation was up and running.

He exited the email from Butcher and went through the others, which consisted mostly of spam. He ran across a status email from John Callahan, the private detective CJ had hired to find the bastard who had robbed him. Still, no progress in locating Bill Reynolds. CJ wasn't surprised, but he still felt disappointed at the news. Like he'd figured early on, Reynolds and the money were no doubt long gone.

CJ checked the time and saw it was after 1:00 p.m., around

the time Jillian usually took lunch, and her employees or one of her sisters covered for her. He located her in his favorites and pressed *Send*.

It rang three times before Jillian answered with a breathless, "Hi, CJ."

"Hey, beautiful." He leaned back in his chair. "Did I catch you at a bad time?"

"Not at all." Jillian had a smile in her voice. "I was just giving Rae an order for delivery. Leeann is covering for me while I'm at lunch."

CJ got up, phone to his ear, and carried his plate to the dishwasher. "How's your day going?"

"Great." Jillian sounded pleased. "We've had a busy Friday morning, and it hadn't let up until about thirty or so minutes ago. Business has been steady since I opened the store's front door."

"I'm proud of you." The plate clinked against another as CJ slid it into the dishwasher. "You put your mind to it, and you made your dream a reality."

"So far, so good." She let out a happy sigh. "How is your day going?"

"Busy." He shut the dishwasher door. "The corrals are officially ready, same for the pastures."

"Fantastic." A pause. "Hold on a sec."

CJ walked to his home office as he heard muffled conversation.

Jillian returned. "Sorry. Leeann had a question for a customer. You're going to an auction tomorrow, right?"

"Yep." He eased into his comfortable executive office chair. "Eight, sharp."

"Good luck getting your cattle at a good price," she said. "How many are you planning to buy?"

He leaned back, the chair squeaking with the movement.

"Around thirty head. Should be enough to get this place going. I'll add to my herd when I'm ready."

"Are you planning to hire anyone to help?"

"I'll probably hire a 4-H kid to muck out stalls once I get too busy to do it myself. For now, I should be able to handle it." He switched the conversation away from his ranch. "Are you free on Sunday?"

"It's Grandpa Daniel's 99th birthday," Jillian said. "The party is at noon at Carter's place. Would you like to go? I meant to ask you earlier, but the week has gotten away from me. You can bring Sadie, if you'd like. The grandkids would love her to pieces."

He appreciated how Jillian always wanted to include the puppy when possible. "Sadie and I would be happy to join you and your family for the party. How about we pick you up?"

"That would be great," Jillian said. "Eleven-forty good with you?"

"Sounds great." He smiled. "It'll be good to catch up with the rest of your family. I've only seen Carter and your sisters since I've been back. Your mom and dad were like a second set of parents to me way back when Carter, Colt, and I were in high school. I'm sorry I won't be seeing your Grandma Francis."

"We miss her." Jillian sounded a little more subdued. "She was the best. We only had her and Grandpa Daniel as grandparents when we were kids. Mom's parents died before Carter was born."

"My grandparents have been gone for many years," CJ said. "I was pretty young by the time we lost all but my Grandma Katheryn. She was tough, and I couldn't put a toe out of line without getting my butt put in a corner. But I loved her like crazy, and it hurt a lot when she was gone."

"I've always been closest to my Grandpa Daniel, probably more than my brothers and sisters have been." Jillian had a smile in her voice again. "He's always been there when I've needed him. I told him before anyone else in my family that I wanted to start my own business, and it was his encouragement that helped me find the guts to do it."

"He's a great man," CJ said. "I look forward to seeing him again."

"I'd better run," Jillian said. "I just heard the doorbells jangle three times in a row so that probably means Leeann has her hands full. Have a good day at the auction tomorrow."

CJ smiled, imagining her gorgeous smile. "See you Sunday, beautiful."

"See you both then," she said before she disconnected the call.

He sat for a long moment, thinking about Jillian and looking forward to spending time with her again.

He'd been putting off talking with her about possibly selling the ranch and traveling. This Sunday sounded like a good time to share with her what he was considering doing.

The thought that she would tell him she couldn't see him anymore made his heart ache like nothing he could have imagined. They'd only been dating a few weeks, but she'd gotten inside him so deep that he couldn't imagine not having her in his life.

"Sadie, love." Jillian knelt and hugged the puppy on the threshold of her home. "Just you wait—you're going to have the time of your life with the McLeod rugrats."

CJ grinned as he watched his girlfriend greet his dog before even saying hello to him.

Sadie licked Jillian's cheek, and she giggled before rising and looping her hands around CJ's neck. "I've missed you this week."

He breathed in her honeysuckle scent as he nuzzled the top of her head. "You always smell so damn good."

CJ raised his head and smiled at her as she tipped her chin up and met his gaze. "Then kiss me, fool."

He chuckled and obliged. She tasted so sweet and delicious that he didn't want to stop. When he did, she looked as out of breath as he felt.

Jillian picked up a covered bowl, and he took it from her and carried it onto the porch. "What's in here?"

"German potato salad." She locked the door behind her. "Everyone asks for it at family events, so I usually make it."

"Sounds delicious."

They walked down the porch steps of her home, Sadie chasing their heels. The dog's herding instinct still had her trying to herd her people, too. He'd train her to stick to cattle, but she was bound to enjoy trying to round up the McLeod children today.

When Sadie was safe in her crate, and he and Jillian had buckled themselves in, CJ put the truck into gear and headed out of the neighborhood and on toward the highway.

"It's been such a crazy week." Jillian blew out her breath. "I love that it has been busy since opening day, so I'm not complaining."

He glanced at her. "You're one hell of a businesswoman."

"I'm trying." She smiled at him. "I know I'm a good accountant, so that helps. And I think coming from a large family makes it easier to talk to people." She gave a little laugh. "Can't hurt having lived in this community all my life, and our family is well known and well respected."

"When it comes down to it, it's all about you." He looked from the road to her. "Own it."

She gave him another smile and relaxed in her seat, and he

looked back to the highway. "I really appreciate your support, CJ. It means a lot to me."

He guided the truck onto the highway. "I say it like I see it."

"Thank you," she said quietly.

He got into the left lane to pass a tractor, which reminded him of the accident he'd come across and meeting the man named Dave Ross, who was probably Mindy's ex. He hadn't thought of either of them until now.

He pulled the truck back into the right lane as he mulled over the differences between the girl he'd known way back when and Jillian. Those differences seemed even stronger now that he'd gotten to know Jillian better, and she came out on top by a mile.

Jillian cut into his thoughts. "How was the auction?"

"I bought twenty-seven head of cattle." He spotted the exit to the road that led to Carter's ranch. "They're being delivered later this week."

"That's great." Jillian had a lilt of enthusiasm in her tone. "It'll feel more like a ranch once you have your herd."

He nodded. "It'll be good to be back in business."

"How big do you plan to build your operation?" she asked.

He kept his gaze focused on the road. Now wasn't the time to tell her what he'd been considering doing. The time for that would be when they were at dinner alone or some other time when they were sitting together and relaxed. Not when they were driving and headed to spend time with her family.

When they finally drove up to Carter's sprawling home, the parking lot was filled with close to ten vehicles.

"Is this all family, or are friends here, too?" CJ parked between a black truck and a red SUV.

"Our get-togethers are usually just family." She flashed him a grin. "There are more than enough of us. There's not much room to add too many to the equation."

Carter's Border Collie, Lucy, came out to meet them, her butt wiggling in greeting.

CJ opened Jillian's door and helped her out, then let Sadie down.

Lucy barked, then sniffed Sadie, and the puppy scampered around, excited to meet another dog.

Sadie and Jillian walked with CJ as he carried the potato salad to the front door. Lucy took off around the side of the house.

The moment Jillian opened the door, the sound of laughter and chatter met their ears. She took the bowl from him, and he closed the door behind him before following her into the crowded kitchen.

"Hi, Mom." Jillian set the bowl on the island and hugged a tall, slim woman with dark hair shot through with silver.

"You look as lovely as ever, Mrs. McLeod." CJ extended his hand to her.

She beamed at him, ignored his hand, and hugged him. "You're old enough to call me Julie, CJ."

He grinned at her as they parted. "It's good to see you."

Jillian introduced her to Kit, Carter's wife, a pretty woman with butterscotch-colored hair and moss-green eyes.

"Welcome, CJ." Kit hugged him. "Carter has told me some interesting stories that involve you and Colt."

CJ smiled. "Hopefully, not all the stories."

"Probably not." She motioned to identical twin girls. "Emily, Olivia, come meet your daddy's old high school friend, CJ."

The girls stood in front of him and one of the girls held out her hand, and she had an energetic, outgoing nature. "I'm Emily. Nice to meet you."

He took her small hand in his. "Pleasure's all mine, Emily." He held out his hand to Olivia. "It's a pleasure to meet you as well, Olivia."

Olivia looked more solemn as she shook his hand.

He straightened. "How old are you two?"

Emily promptly spoke up. "We're eight."

He smiled at Emily and then Olivia. "You are lovely young ladies."

"Thank you," Emily said.

Olivia nodded, then said, "Can I pet your puppy?"

"You sure can. Her name is Sadie." He stepped aside.

The girls fell on the Aussie at once. Sadie wiggled her butt and licked their faces.

Emily and Olivia giggled.

Kit motioned to the French doors leading to the back porch. "Go on now and take the puppy outside where there's more room. Your cousins would love to meet Sadie, too."

"Can I help with anything?" Jillian asked Kit.

CJ followed the young girls and the puppy through the French doors and onto the back porch.

The next thing he knew, a passel of kids surrounded Sadie. Emily introduced him to five-year-old Jacob and his sister, two-year-old Karley, Justin and Miranda's children. Then there was Bear and Rae's three-and-a-half-year-old, Jeremiah, and Colt and Marlee's daughter, Charlotte, who was almost two.

A composed and pretty girl he recognized as Kaycee from the rodeo introduced herself and her boyfriend, Tatum. "My Uncle Carter said you're Aunt Jillian's boyfriend."

He smiled at Kaycee. "Congratulations on winning the barrel racing championship at the youth rodeo during the Spring Fling. Your aunt and I watched you race. You're an excellent rider."

Kaycee dimpled. "Thank you."

CJ held out his hand to Tatum. "You are something else on bareback. Congrats on your win."

Tatum gave a nod. "Thank you kindly, sir."

"Call me CJ." He released the young man's hand. "What are your plans after graduation?"

"University of Arizona Rodeo Team." Tatum put his arm around Kaycee's shoulders. "The school offered scholarships to each of us."

"Great job," CJ told them. "After seeing you both ride, I'm not surprised."

He talked with the pair a while longer about rodeo before Jillian joined them and also congratulated the pair.

"Colt is grilling." Jillian nodded in that direction. "Come on and say hello."

CJ and Jillian walked across the lawn, past a collection of picnic tables, to the grill, where Colt and Carter were talking. Wood smoke and the smells of the grilling steaks filled the air.

"The team is back together again." Colt slapped CJ's shoulder. "Been far too long."

"Don't know where the time has gone." CJ took the beer that Carter handed him from a cooler.

Jillian waved away the beer Carter offered her. "Mom said she's making margaritas, so I'm holding out for the good stuff." She backed away. "Speaking of her, I'm going to see if she needs help."

The can felt cold in CJ's hands. He pulled the tab and took a healthy swallow.

"Marlee mentioned she met you at the fairgrounds during Spring Fling," Colt said. "I hope you and Jillian will take us up on the offer to join us for dinner."

"I'll look forward to it." CJ nodded. "While Jillian's getting her business off the ground, Sundays are best."

"We're mighty proud of our little sister," Carter said. "Always thought she was meant for bigger things."

Colt raised his beer in agreement. "Jillian has a good head on her shoulders."

CJ enjoyed catching up with his old best friends. "I've met your wives and kids, and you've done well for yourselves."

"Can't complain." Carter smiled fondly in the direction of the children, who were still playing with the puppy. "Life's been good to us."

"I hear you're getting your ranch up and running," Colt said when Carter left to refill the ice chest with more sodas and drinks. "I haven't heard the story about why you're having to rebuild your parents' operation."

Trying to keep his temper in control, CJ explained about the foreman. Just speaking about what the bastard had done caused his scalp to burn.

"It's a real shame." Colt shook his head. "I hope your PI finds him, and you can recoup at least some of what you've lost."

CJ shrugged. "By this time, I doubt it, but you never know."

Jillian showed up at his side again. "Grandpa Daniel is here. Haylee and Tyson just brought him." Jillian took his hand. "Come on and say hello."

"Catch you later," CJ said to Colt.

JILLIAN TOOK CJ by the hand and led him to where her grandfather reclined in an Adirondack chair. Justin had given the elderly man a beer as they'd seated him.

Her heart twisted to see how much he'd aged over the past year. Her grandpa had always been larger than life. Now, he trembled when he walked, and his once steady hands shook. But he was still sharp and intelligent.

She took the chair on the elderly man's right and rested her hand on his. "Grandpa, do you remember CJ Jameson?"

"I certainly do." Grandpa Daniel started to rise to greet him.

"Don't get up on account of me." CJ took a seat on Grandpa's left. "It's good to see you, Mr. McLeod."

Grandpa Daniel settled back in his chair. "Still in the service, young man?"

CJ shook his head. "Honorable discharge when I shattered both legs in a parachuting accident. So, I'm now getting my parents' ranch back in business."

"Admirable." Grandpa gave a nod. "Your mama will be sorely missed. She was a lovely woman."

"That she was." CJ looked a little wistful. "I didn't come back enough. Time always seemed to get away."

Grandpa patted CJ's hand. "Your mama was right proud of you."

CJ smiled. "I'm a lucky man to have had parents like mine. Like your family is to have each other."

"I've always counted myself as blessed many times over." Grandpa gave a contented smile and patted Jillian's hand this time. His touch was warm and dry. "My Jillian here is one of my greatest blessings."

Jillian leaned over and kissed Grandpa Daniel's cheek. "You do know you're my favorite, don't you?"

He chuckled. "How's business going, pumpkin?"

"Great." Jillian leaned forward, resting her folded arms on her knees. "Having learned integrity in everything I do from you is one of the most important lessons you taught me from a young age."

Grandpa nodded. "Your sisters still giving you a hand?"

"Talk about blessings." Jillian settled back in her chair. "Leeann and Haylee have both been there for me, and even my sisters-in-law have pitched in. I don't know what I would have done without them. Business is going well enough that I'm going to hire an employee in addition to the young lady who does deliveries for me. I'll start interviewing this week."

"I'm not surprised you're doing such a fine job," Grandpa said.

Kaycee approached and smiled. "Hi, Great-Grandpa. I've been sent to fetch you all for dinner."

"My belly's been hollerin' since I got here." Grandpa started to push himself out of his chair, and CJ hurried to assist him.

After seating Grandpa at a picnic table, Jillian headed for the food. She passed a shorter picnic table where the kids who were old enough to eat on their own sat. Kaycee and Tatum sat at the same table as Justin and Miranda and their little ones. Kaycee often served as babysitter to many of the McLeod offspring. Jillian wondered how they were all going to manage without her once she went on to the university.

A large folding table had been erected and now brimmed with bowls of green salad, macaroni and potato salads, baked beans, relish trays, tortilla and potato chips, and platters of hot dogs, hamburgers, and steaks.

Jillian filled Grandpa's plate and carried it to him, along with napkins and plastic utensils, before going back for her own. CJ got another beer while Jillian went for the pitcher of margaritas. After loading their own plates, they sat with Grandpa.

Bear and Rae joined them. Rae looked at their little Jeremiah who sat at the kids' table. "He's getting so big." She turned back to everyone. "We decided to try for another. Not sure if we've waited too long, but he's been such a handful."

"That's wonderful." Jillian set down her fork. "Age gap isn't a big deal. Look at our family."

"I know." Rae smiled. "It's always good to see you all together."

They laughed and chatted, and Grandpa Daniel told some of his tall tales that had them laughing.

When they were about finished, Tyson and Haylee stood. She looked so stunning and beautiful that Jillian knew what they were going to announce before Haylee got it out.

"We're going to have a baby," Haylee said to cheers and

shouts of congratulations. When it died down, she added. "He or she is going to be a Christmas baby."

"The best Christmas gift I can imagine," Tyson said as he rested his arm around Haylee's shoulders. "Other than my beautiful wife."

More cheers until the couple returned to their seats.

Jillian's dad, Joe, stood and raised his hand. "Now, for the reason we are all here." He gestured to Grandpa Daniel. "To the finest man I've ever known, my dad."

Applause and shouts of agreement from all around. Then Kit and Julie came through the French doors, carrying a huge cake that Kit had baked, and Julie had decorated. On top were two candles in the shapes of nines.

Everyone broke out singing "Happy Birthday, dear Grandpa," and more cheers as the cake was set in front of him. He paused only a moment before he blew them out.

"What did you wish for, Great-Grandpa?" Emily asked.

Grandpa smiled. "I have lived a long life, and right here, I have everything a man could wish for surrounding him. My wish is for you to have all that I have been fortunate enough to be gifted with."

A tear rolled down Jillian's cheek. His words made her realize even more how much she'd been blessed with in her relatively short life. She saw CJ watching her, and she turned to him and smiled. And now she had a man she was head-over-heels in love with, and all that she could desire was to have him in her life forever.

Smiling, he put his hand over hers, and she wondered if he felt the way she did.

She turned to her grandpa, who beamed as Kit gave him the first piece of cake. It was red velvet, his favorite, and Jill's.

"I love you, Grandpa," she said.

He patted her shoulder. "I love you, my darling Jill."

Her chest tightened as she saw how tired he was, how much this party had already taken out of him.

Then he sat up straighter and smiled, and she saw a ghost of the vibrant man he'd once been.

She leaned over, hugged him, and breathed in his Old Spice cologne scent before parting and smiling at CJ. He rested his arm around her shoulders, and warmth traveled through her, giving her a sense of happiness and peace.

———

9

Jillian parked her Ford in front of CJ's home, excitement over spending the day with him filling her chest with warmth. He stepped out of the front door and jogged down the steps, Sadie at his side, and her heart fluttered. He looked so sexy and handsome that he took her breath away. She hadn't realized just how much she'd missed him until that moment.

He'd had a busy week since Grandpa Daniel's birthday party, and he hadn't had time to come into town to go out to lunch like he usually did. Today was the first chance they'd had to spend time together since the party.

CJ reached her door and opened it before Jillian could. "Hello, beautiful." He took her hand, helped her out of her SUV, and looked down at her, the corners of his mouth turned up in a sensual smile.

"Hi," she said breathlessly before he embraced her and lowered his mouth to hers. He took his time, moving his lips over hers, then sliding his tongue between her lips, and kissing her until her mind spun.

He drew back and held her gaze. "I'm glad you could make it out today."

"I've been looking forward to it all week." She stepped aside as he shut the SUV's door behind her. "Time is passing by much too quickly, yet it never seems fast enough when it comes to spending time with you."

"I don't like going so long without seeing you." He stood in front of her, studying her, and pushed hair away from her face and behind her ear with his fingers. "One weekend soon, you'll need to get someone to cover for you so that I can whisk you away to get you all to myself for more than just a day at a time."

"I like that idea." Her words came out husky, and she wondered if she sounded as wanton to him as she did to herself. "But give me a few more weeks. I need to train my staff and make sure everything is running smoothly before I take a whole weekend off."

"I understand." The corner of his mouth quirked. "That doesn't mean I have to be patient about it."

Jillian laughed, then crouched and greeted the puppy, who licked her nose and caused her to giggle. She got to her feet. "Sadie has gotten so big."

CJ looked fondly at the Aussie. "She's grown so fast I have a hard time remembering what she looked like when I got her."

Jillian opened the rear door of her SUV and gestured to the two pizza boxes on the back seat. "I've had to smell these all the way out here, and I'm starving."

He grabbed the boxes and shut the vehicle's door before heading to the house, keeping his strides shorter so she could keep up. Smells of ham and pineapple from one pizza and sausage and pepperoni from the other accompanied them.

The screen door squawked as CJ opened it and held it wide so that Jillian and Sadie could precede him.

Jillian felt comfortable in his home, which he'd furnished in a mixture of southwestern and Native American décor. Over the past several weeks, he'd redecorated, reminding her more and more of a hunting lodge where one would snuggle up while a snowstorm raged outside. Considering they were in Central Arizona, not too far removed from Phoenix, a snowstorm would be rare indeed. But they could snuggle up on a rainy day, and that was just as good.

His kitchen was old-fashioned but filled with all the necessary modern conveniences. He set the pizza boxes on the kitchen island, where he'd already placed a pizza cutter on the butcher block surface.

She opened one of the boxes to reveal the Hawaiian pizza. "Do you cook much for yourself?"

He shrugged as he took a couple of plates out of a cabinet. "I usually keep it simple for myself. In the service, I didn't do much entertaining."

She smiled at him. "And then it was probably pizza and beer for the boys?"

"And female Airmen who joined us as well." He cast her a grin. "I ordered plenty of pizzas just for myself, too."

Jillian nodded. "I like to cook, but Leeann prefers to do ours. I think it's another way for her to be creative, so I don't argue." Jillian sighed as she leaned her hip against a counter. "As tired as I've been after work since opening the store, I'm truly thrilled she's been taking care of it all."

He gestured to the pizzas. "Which do you prefer?"

"Pineapple and ham is my favorite, so two of those." She moved to the fridge. "Beer?"

"Yep. I have a six-pack chilled and ready." He loaded one plate with two slices of Hawaiian, then slid three slices of pepperoni and sausage onto his own plate. "Crushed red pepper and parmesan?"

Jillian grabbed a couple of cans of beer. "Plenty of both."

CJ shook liberal amounts of the peppers and parmesan on all slices. Jillian tore off two paper towels from a roll and folded them to use as napkins. Sadie trotted at her heels as she carried them with the beer to CJ's TV room in the back of the house.

It was a comfortable room in earth tones and rich oak furnishings, with two overstuffed recliners and a comfy couch. The TV room furniture was a little scuffed but in good condition, unlike the front room furniture, which was brand new. Sadie curled up in a doggie bed near the base of the eighty-five-inch screen TV.

CJ and Jillian sat close on the couch, and CJ stretched out his legs beneath the coffee table. He turned on the TV and switched channels to the Arizona vs San Diego Padres pregame show. The game was in San Diego, so the Diamondbacks would be first up to bat.

Sitting so close to CJ on the couch felt comfortable as their bodies touched from their thighs to their shoulders. Jillian had never felt so completely at ease with a man, and her heart had never felt so full.

"The Diamondbacks are starting out so well now that we're into the regular season." Jillian picked up a slice of Hawaiian as CJ took a slug of beer. "It would be great if they make it all the way to the World Series again."

He set down his beer. "And even better if they don't choke this time."

Jillian nodded as she chewed her bite. She swallowed and followed that with a drink of beer. "With us cheering them on together, how can they lose?"

"Of course." CJ chuckled. "Our fandom makes the difference."

They munched on their pizza while enjoying the baseball game. Jillian didn't know if she'd ever felt so relaxed or content. She was keenly aware of him next to her, and during lulls in the game, she couldn't help but wish she was in his lap kissing him, everything else bedamned.

As the game went on, they were up and down in their seats, cheering for good plays and shouting at the refs for bad calls.

One play after another grew more intense when they reached the ninth inning, and they were both on the edge of their seats, the score tied three to three. With two outs, the Diamondbacks hit a one-run base hit to take the lead before striking out.

The bottom of the ninth with the Padres at-bat was a nail-biter. Their big hitter sent what looked like a home run to the back wall. A Diamondback's outfielder jumped impossibly high, his hand stretched out, and he caught the ball with the tip of his glove for a hard-won out and for the win.

CJ and Jillian jumped to their feet, cheering and high-fiving. Then, with the sound of hyped-up commentators in the background, CJ took Jillian into his arms and kissed her.

The kiss was as intense as the moment, and she answered it with all the excitement she'd been feeling—but the excitement of being in his arms meant more than the entire game.

The kiss continued until her mind spun, and she felt breathless and dizzy, her skin flushed and warm. At that moment, she knew she was ready to take their relationship further. She didn't want to waste a second more to know him in the most intimate way a woman could know a man.

When they finally parted, his eyes looked impossibly dark, his chest rising and falling as much as hers. His throat worked as he visibly swallowed. "Jillian." Her name came out as a husky croak.

She pressed her body tightly to his. "Yes." She put into that word all the meaning she could. *Yes,* I'm ready. *Yes,* I want you. But she couldn't quite get all the words out.

His expression clouded, which took her aback. "I need to talk with you."

She searched his gaze, wondering why he suddenly looked so serious.

Before she could respond, her cell phone rang. She hesitated, not wanting CJ to think she'd put a call before him. But he gave her a nod and a decisive, "Take it."

She looked at the screen and saw that it was her mother. She answered the phone with, "Hi, Mom."

"Jill, honey." Her mom sounded like her words were choked. "It's Grandpa Daniel. He's in the hospital, and it doesn't look good. You should come now."

Jillian felt like a bucket of ice water had been poured over her. "Not Grandpa." She clenched the phone tighter. "King Creek Hospital?"

"Yes."

"I'm on my way." Jillian disconnected the call and met CJ's gaze, her face frozen. "It's my grandpa. He's in the hospital."

"I'll take you." CJ wrapped his arm around her shoulders as they hurried to the kitchen, where she grabbed her purse.

Sadie followed them, and CJ put her in her kennel since she was still just a puppy, and he made sure she had water.

Jillian felt the urge to run as fast as she could to get away from the fear and the pain. He had lived a good, long life, but as irrational as the thought was, she'd felt like he would be here forever.

They went in CJ's truck. She didn't feel like talking on the drive to the hospital, a ball of dread firmly lodged in her throat, and CJ remained quiet, too.

When they got to the hospital, CJ escorted her through the front entrance and to the information desk. The receptionist looked up her grandfather's name and told them what room he was in.

CJ didn't have to shorten his stride because Jillian hurried the entire way. When they reached Grandpa's room, she came to a full stop, afraid to go in.

Jillian couldn't move until CJ rested his palm on her shoulder. "Are you all right?"

She shook her head, fighting back tears. She'd known the day would come, but that didn't make it any easier.

CJ squeezed her shoulder, then guided her in through the open door.

Her parents, Joe and Julie McLeod, were at Grandpa's side, and her dad's face was etched with concern. Her mom was pale as she got up from the chair beside the bed.

"You're the first to arrive." Julie beckoned her in. "Grandpa has been asking for you, but he's asleep now."

Jillian felt like she was slogging through mud as she forced herself forward. She eased into the chair and took her grandfather's cold hand in hers.

His eyelids fluttered, and he turned his head and looked at her. "Pumpkin, there you are." His voice rasped like sandpaper on wood.

The backs of Jillian's eyelids prickled as she struggled not to cry. She gripped his hand tighter. "Hi, Grandpa."

"I'm not long for this world, my girl." He spoke slowly as if he was struggling to speak. "I'm glad I have the chance to tell you how proud I am of you and how much I love you."

"You mean so much to me." Jillian couldn't help the tears that now flowed freely down her cheeks. "I love you, Grandpa."

He gripped her hand as he looked up at CJ. "Young man, take care of my girl."

CJ moved closer and rested his palm on Jillian's shoulder. "I will, sir."

Grandpa smiled weakly. "I'll go easier knowing she has someone who loves her like I do."

Jillian stiffened, her scalp prickling as she avoided looking at CJ and kept her gaze on her grandfather.

"Yes, sir," CJ said in a low but confident tone and gripped Jillian's shoulder tighter.

Did he really love her, or was he just telling an old man on his deathbed what he wanted to hear?

Her throat worked as she swallowed. "I don't want you to go, Grandpa."

He reached over with his other hand, which was attached to the IV, and he patted the top of hers. "I've lived a good, long life, pumpkin. I'm going to see your Grandma Francis soon. I have sorely missed her."

Jillian nodded as tears rolled down her cheeks and onto her shirt. "Tell her hello for me."

He patted her hand again. "I will."

The sound of voices came from behind Jillian, and she looked up to see Haylee, Leeann, Brady, and Carter slipping into the room.

Jillian squeezed Grandpa's hand. "I love you," she said again, and he smiled.

She got up from the chair and let her siblings say their good-byes. Justin, Colt, and Bear soon followed. Their spouses stayed outside the room, and she realized CJ had left, too.

Bear was the last to hold Grandpa's hand, and he swept his gaze around, looking at all the faces of his loved ones. "I love you all," he said before closing his eyes, his face going slack.

The heart monitor flatlined and made a piercing noise.

Jillian stared at him, willing him to open his eyes and speak again, proving the heart monitor to be wrong. But he didn't move, and his chest had stopped rising and falling.

A nurse came in and turned off the monitor. She took Grandpa's wrist and held it before looking at the clock. She lowered his hand and rested it on the bed. "He's gone."

A scream rose up within Jillian, and she wanted to shout at them to start his heart pumping again. But he'd told the family long ago that he had a DNR and was not to be resuscitated when the time came.

She suddenly couldn't breathe. She pushed her way through her family members and outside the room and strode down the hallway as fast as she could, needing air and time to pull herself together. She reached the double doors to the waiting room before realizing CJ was at her side.

He took her hand, and she turned to face him, tears pouring, her chest aching as if someone had knocked the wind out of her. "I can't believe he's gone." Her words came out in a near whisper. "I've always felt like he'd be around forever."

CJ took her into his embrace and held her to him as her body shook with sobs. He spoke in a low, soothing tone. "He'll always be with you, Jillian. He'll always be in your heart."

She tipped her head back to look at him. "How do you move on from so much pain?"

He gave her a gentle smile. "You don't move on. You move forward, taking him and your memories with you."

She rested her head against his chest, trying to control her tears. "I'm going to miss him so much."

"It'll take a while, but eventually, it will get easier." CJ slowly rubbed her back. "Trust me. I've lost my mom and my dad. I wish I could have said goodbye to them, but I was far away when each of them passed."

Jillian let out a long, shuddering sigh. "At least I got to tell him I love him before he was gone."

CJ stroked her hair. "And you got to hear him tell you how much he loved you."

She nodded and realized his shirt was partially damp from her tears. She looked up at him again. "I want to go somewhere. I don't want—I don't want to see him when he's not really there anymore." Her throat worked. "I don't know if they'll understand why I'm leaving."

"I think they will." He slid his fingers through her hair again. "But if you want to go back and let them know, we can do that."

She looked over her shoulder at the crowd now outside Grandpa's room, then back to CJ. "No, I just want to go."

He wrapped his arm around her shoulders and led her through the double doors, and the waiting room, then down the hall, past the receptionist, and out to his truck.

They drove to Founders Park, and once they'd left his vehicle, they walked hand-in-hand to the kids' playground. Jillian sat on one of the swings and gripped the cool chains to either side of her. She slowly moved back and forth, not swinging, her feet dragging through the dirt, lost in thought and memory.

After a while, she looked up to see CJ leaning against one of the swing set's poles, watching her. The day was warm, but a cool breeze smelling of grass and spring blossoms caught her hair and blew it across her face. She brushed it away with her fingers.

"I was sad when we lost Grandma Francis a couple of years ago," she said quietly. "I don't know why, but it didn't hit me as hard as Grandpa's death." Tears pricked her eyes again. "Maybe I do. I loved Grandma, but I was much closer to Grandpa. We talked on the phone fairly often, and I went out to their ranch to visit with him, especially after Grandma passed away."

CJ listened, his gaze focused on hers. "From what he said, I think he felt the same closeness to you."

She nodded slowly. "I know my siblings love him as much as I do, but I spent more time with him than anyone else, except maybe for my dad." She smiled wistfully. "We used to go on rides together, up to the Superstitions, and we'd have picnics. Sometimes, we'd go fishing at the lake."

"You didn't get a chance to meet my new Quarter Horse,

Molly." CJ smiled at her. "What do you say to riding up to the mountains sometime soon? You can say goodbye to your grandpa there, too."

"I like that idea." She tipped her head to the side. "I can show you where we used to picnic. Do you like to fish?"

"I do." He rolled his shoulders. "I'll have to buy some fishing tackle—what my mom and dad had all disappeared along with everything else."

She shook her head. "I don't have any—we always used Grandpa's stuff. You don't have to buy any on my account."

"I'd like to get some gear regardless." He moved and sat in the swing next to hers. "I have lots of good memories of fishing with my dad."

She gripped the chains of her swing. "It's a date."

He nodded. "I'll get a couple of fishing licenses along with the tackle, and we'll be all set."

She smiled, but then her lips trembled as her thoughts turned back to Grandpa. She leaned back in her swing and kicked off. She swung back and forth, higher and higher. The wind in her hair and on her face made her feel lighter, if only for that moment in time.

Memories of time spent with Grandpa filled her heart not just with pain but the love she felt for him. She looked at the park's trees, paths, and benches as she swung and then rooftops of the neighborhood on the other side of the park. Marlee used to live there before she and Colt married.

She looked to her side and saw CJ swinging, too. He had a boyish expression like he was enjoying himself. Maybe, despite her loss, she was, too.

Her energy started draining away, and she let the swing slow until her feet skimmed the ground. Gradually, she halted, her shoes resting on the dry soil. CJ came to a stop beside her, and their gazes met and held.

She voiced her concern again. "Do you think my family understands why I left?"

He nodded. "Everyone grieves in their own way. They know how much you loved your grandpa, and I'm sure they know how close you two were."

"Mom and Dad have commented on it before." Jillian sighed. "I think they were glad that we did have such a good relationship, especially after Grandma passed."

CJ stood in front of her and held out his hands, and she took them, allowing him to bring her to her feet. "Would you like to go back?"

She looked at the ground and thought about it before meeting his gaze again. "I'll call Mom." She released his hands, pulled her phone out of her pocket, and then dialed her mom from her *Favorites* menu. She brought her phone to her ear.

"Hi, Jill dear," Mom said when she answered. "Are you all right?"

Even though her mom couldn't see her, Jillian nodded. "I'll be okay. I'm at the park with CJ because I need some time alone. Do you want me to come back?"

"You take some time to yourself." Her mom's understanding tone made Jillian's heart feel a little better. "I'll call you tomorrow. We'll need to plan your grandfather's memorial. I think we know where to get the flowers."

"I think you do." Jillian let out her breath. "I love you, Mom."

"I love you, honey."

Jillian disconnected the call and slid her phone into her pocket. Her chest still hurt, and she had a feeling it would be that way for a while.

CJ clasped her hand, guiding her back across the park toward his truck. "Would you like me to drive you home? We can figure out how to get your car to you tomorrow."

She shook her head. "I'm fine driving, and I'll need my SUV in the morning."

"We can have the rest of the pizza for dinner, or I can whip up something else," he said.

"Leftover pizza sounds good." She looked up at him. "I don't want to be alone, but I won't stay late."

He brought her to a stop by the passenger side door. "Stay as long as you'd like."

"It will be good to hug Sadie." She tipped her head up and looked into his eyes. "Speaking of hugs..."

He brought her into his embrace and held her close, and she felt his heartbeat against her ear. It was a slow, comforting beat that somehow made her feel better. When they drew apart, he gave her a soft kiss before helping her into her seat and closing the door behind her.

As he walked around, she leaned her head back and thought about the day. She'd been so excited to spend time with CJ, then had crashed so low when Grandpa Daniel passed. Now, she felt a dull ache in her chest, but at least she wasn't crying. Her eyes still burned and felt puffy and swollen, but for the time being, she was all cried out.

When they were on their way, she looked out the window at the scenery whipping by. So many thoughts crowded her mind, mostly about her last moments with her grandpa. Then she remembered what he'd said to CJ about taking care of her and him being glad she had someone to love her like he had. Heat flushed through her body as she wondered what had gone through his mind.

Jillian was in love with CJ, but she didn't know how he felt about her. Maybe Grandpa had seen something that she hadn't. She'd just have to let time play out, and then she'd know. Sooner rather than later, she hoped.

10

The memorial was two weeks after Grandpa was cremated. Jillian's heart ached. She thought about him every day and found herself tearing up every time a memory came back to her. CJ had been so supportive and there for her.

A week after the memorial, on the first Sunday in June, Jillian drove out to CJ's ranch and parked in front of his home.

Talk about handsome—he was in a forest-green T-shirt, Wranglers, and boots as he and Sadie met her at her SUV. He opened the door. "You sure look cute."

"Thanks." Jillian took his hand and stepped out. She wore jeans, a royal blue T-shirt, boots, and a baseball cap with her ponytail through the back opening.

She knelt to hug the Aussie before CJ put her in the kennel inside his home. It wasn't safe for a puppy to be out due to coyotes living in the area. According to CJ, once Sadie was a little older, she could accompany him on rides and while working with cattle. Her training was progressing well, and her herding instinct was strong.

"Everything is ready." CJ took the soft-sided cooler with the lunch she'd prepared for their fishing trip off her back seat.

They strode toward the barn, CJ carrying the cooler while his herd lowed from the pasture. He'd purchased Hereford cattle that had the characteristic red bodies with white faces and underbellies.

He shifted the cooler in his grip. "I bought our fishing licenses."

"Great," Jillian said. "Thanks for doing that."

The day was already starting to warm. In Central Arizona, June's average temperature was in the mid-100s, and today would be no exception.

"I've been looking forward to this trip since we first talked about it." Jillian followed him inside the dim, cool barn.

He'd saddled the horses shortly before she arrived. "The rancher I bought Molly from said she's a gentle mare and doesn't spook easily. Faith is a little more headstrong, so I'll take her. I've worked with Molly over the past three weeks, and I think she'll be a good ride for you."

Jillian stroked Molly's neck and spoke quietly to her. "We'll get along famously."

CJ put the fishing tackle, including collapsible rods, and the cooler with their lunch into the saddlebags. He also included another soft-sided cooler, this one filled with ice for the trout.

"You are such a beautiful girl," she said to the black Quarter Horse that had a blaze and white socks. "We're going to have a lovely ride today."

After she spoke to Molly for a bit, Jillian put her left boot into the stirrup, then swung her right leg over and mounted the mare. It had been a while since she had ridden, and she felt exhilarated to be in the saddle again. Sitting so high and feeling the powerful animal shift beneath her was a heady sensation.

When CJ finished preparations, he climbed into his own saddle atop Faith and smiled at Jillian. "Ready for some fun?"

She beamed at him in return. "I am *so* ready."

CJ clicked his tongue, and Faith started forward. Jillian encouraged Molly to follow, and they headed for the pasture gate. He dismounted and opened it, let the mares pass, then closed it before mounting his horse again.

The cloudless sky was as blue as a piece of azure crystal, stretching over their heads for miles. The air smelled clean, of dried grasses, creosote, horse, and the leather of Molly's saddle. Warm air brushed her cheeks as the horses' hooves clopped along the path leading to the Superstition Mountains.

She held the reins loosely as the mare plodded along the path bordered by mesquite, palo verde trees, and cacti. "Have you gone fishing since you came back to live in King Creek?"

He shook his head. "It's been a long while since I've fished in Arizona. I went on trips with my friends while I was in the service. But there's nothing like casting a line in the Superstition Springs Lake." It was a small man-made lake, not that much bigger than a pond, but he'd had some great times there in his childhood and as an adult.

She sighed. "Grandpa and I last went well over a year ago. We had a great time and came home with a cooler full of Rainbow trout that we gutted at the lake. We fried it up with cornmeal, and it was delicious."

CJ glanced from the trail to Jillian. "Can't wait to get it in the pan."

She looked ahead as they entered the foothills, passing by brittlebush, chollas, prickly pear, ocotillos, yuccas, and catclaw trees. A jackrabbit bolted across their path, and a red-tailed hawk circled overhead.

The higher they traveled, the denser and greener the vegetation grew, including ironwood, oak, pinon, and pine trees.

"How are you holding up?" CJ looked at her with concern in his gaze. "Are you still having a hard time with your grandfather's passing?"

"I think about him all the time." Her throat felt crowded as she spoke. "He used to call me to see how I was doing, and I miss hearing his voice." She swallowed past the lump. "But I'm working through it and getting better as time goes by." Their gazes met. "Thank you for helping me get through this."

His gaze held hers. "Any time you need me, I'm here for you."

"Thank you," she said, this time quietly.

An oak branch nearly knocked off CJ's baseball hat, but he clapped his hand on it in time. "Tell me more about your grandpa."

Jillian thought about it. "He grew up in Arizona, his parents coming here from Texas before he was born. He met my grandma when he was twenty, and they married a few months later. They had four sons, all of whom live in the valley surrounding King Creek."

She glanced at CJ before she continued. "My dad was the youngest by ten years, so by the time he was old enough to appreciate his brothers, they'd already moved out. Dad worked so hard to keep the eight of us close since he didn't have the same kind of relationship with his siblings."

"I've known a lot of other McLeods in the area, but not like your immediate family," CJ said. "Except for your cousin, Ellie. Her mom was good friends with my mom, so I saw her every now and then."

"Ellie is my age." Jillian smiled. "She's one of my cousins that my sisters and I are close to." She shrugged. "Everyone is so busy these days that there isn't much time to socialize with extended family."

When CJ asked, Jillian told him stories about her grandpa, and her heart felt lighter with every one of them.

When they reached the small lake, they went to Jillian's favorite tree and laid an old, flowered quilt that he'd brought in a saddlebag beneath it. She set the soft-sided cooler on the quilt and then helped CJ with the fishing tackle.

Some boulders were nearby, close to the water's edge, and they picked two close to each other. CJ took an aluminum stringer and staked the end into the ground at the water's edge.

They put their lightweight poles together, tied hooks onto the fluorocarbon lines, and rigged bobbers and a split shot onto them. They used glittered PowerBait for trout.

"I've never seen the glitter version." Jillian rolled a bit into a ball and slid it onto her hook. "We always used the neon pink stuff or nightcrawlers."

"I've had good luck with this kind in the past." He slid some onto his own hook. "I think it attracts their attention better. Nightcrawlers are excellent, too."

Jillian cast her line, and the wheel made a whirring sound before it plopped into the water a good distance from the shore. She settled onto her rock as CJ cast his own line.

A few minutes after her hook hit the water, the bobber wiggled and then jerked. She got to her feet as the bobber dove below the surface, and her pole bent as the trout tried to take off with the bait.

"I've got one." The thrill that came with fishing sent tingles through her limbs. The trout fought her as she reeled him in. He burst from the surface, his rainbow-colored scales flashing in the light.

"Nice one." CJ's bobber dove beneath the surface, and he started to reel his in. "I think yours is a good nine inches long."

Jillian put the trout on the stringer and removed the hook

with needle nose pliers before putting the stringer with the trout into the water. CJ pulled in his catch and did the same.

They spent the next couple of hours keeping their voices down to avoid scaring off the fish. The sun's rays grew more intense, and CJ produced sunblock, which Jillian rubbed on liberally.

Sparrow and cactus wren calls filled the air, and Jillian caught sight of a brilliant red cardinal as well as a red-capped woodpecker. Colorful hummingbirds darted around the lake's edge. Squirrels and chipmunks scampered in the trees, and lizards scrabbled up and down the bark.

"I'm hungry." Jillian set down her pole after catching her fourth fish and putting it on the stringer with CJ's three. "How about you?"

"Starving." CJ reeled in his line and set aside his pole. "We've done well."

Jillian brushed off her jeans with her palms and walked stiffly to the picnic blanket, where she knelt and unloaded the cooler. "I packed ham and cheddar plus roast beef and Swiss sandwiches." She held up one of each. "Your pick?"

"Both sound good, but I'll go with the roast beef." CJ sat across from her, one long leg stretched out and one knee bent. He took the sandwich she offered and thanked her before opening the bag and taking a big bite. He chewed and swallowed, looking satisfied. "Fantastic. Freshly baked bread, too."

She handed him a small bag of potato chips and a canned soda. "I like to bake on occasion. Glad you like it." She bit into her ham sandwich and had to agree that the bread came out great.

He finished his roast beef, and she gave him a ham and cheese.

When the sandwiches and chips were gone, she offered him a brownie. "I baked these last night."

"You are a good cook." He patted his flat stomach after eating three brownies. "You're going to have to roll me downhill if you keep feeding me like this."

"Someday, I'll make a whole meal for you." She leaned back, bracing her palms on the quilt. "When I'm not so tired from working for six days straight at a time."

"You have been at it hard since you opened your store." He looked at her thoughtfully. "How close are you to taking a whole weekend off?"

She sighed. "I don't know. Maybe I'm being too controlling. I just have a hard time with the idea of not being there every single day. I worry that something will go wrong, and if I go out of town, how would I fix it?"

He cocked his head. "How's your assistant manager turning out?"

"Pretty good." Jillian blew out her breath. "I know that one of these days, I need to let Kristen handle the shop on Saturdays. But when I do, I think I need to stay in town just in case."

CJ gave a slow nod. "Understandable and a smart way to handle it."

She shrugged. "I do need off more than one day a week, though. The business is starting to wear me out. I've been running on adrenaline for months now."

"Why don't you do your trial run next Saturday?" He smiled. "Spend the rest of the day relaxing. If there's an emergency, you'll be close enough to run down to the shop. Then, on Sunday, I'll whisk you away to any place of your choosing."

She gave him a mischievous smile. "Any place?"

"Yep." He nodded. "We could take a day trip to Tucson or the Phoenix area."

She tilted her head to the side. "I saw somewhere that *Chicago,* a Broadway musical that I've wanted to see forever, is playing at the Arizona Broadway Theatre this Saturday."

"Then we'll make it a date." He reached out and ran his finger along her arm, causing a shiver to run through her. "We can go out to dinner afterward."

Her throat worked as she swallowed, and she found it impossible to tear her gaze from his. "All right. I'll find out all the details and let you know."

"Great." He shifted so that he was only inches away. He eased his hand up her arm, and she bit her lower lip as he slid his fingers up the side of her face.

Her heart thumped, and her breathing hitched in her chest. He took off his ballcap then knocked hers off and cupped the back of her head before he lowered his mouth.

She gasped when his lips claimed hers. He kissed her long, slow, and sweet, and she didn't think she'd ever be able to breathe again.

Her entire body started to tremble with need for him. Would he take her now, right on this quilt, under the mountain skies?

When he finally drew away, she stared up into his eyes, unable to think clearly or say a word.

He gently stroked a strand of hair from her cheek. "Ready to do a little more fishing?"

No, she wanted him and not to fish anymore. Instead of voicing that thought aloud, she shrugged and said, "Sure."

He put her hat back on her head, then tugged on his own.

They spent another hour fishing, and then together, they gutted and cleaned the fish before packing it in the ice he'd brought in the second cooler.

Jillian helped him load the saddlebags. "I brought cut-up mixed vegetables to steam, plus cornmeal for the trout and the fixin's to make cornbread for dinner."

"Perfect." He smiled at her. "We'd better get back so you're not out too late."

The ride back to the ranch was just as pleasant as the rest of the day had been. By the end of the ride, she felt dusty and sticky from the sunshine and sunblock.

When they reached his place and got to the barn, they dismounted, and Jillian went into the house to let Sadie out of her kennel. The dog peed and then merrily scampered around Jillian as they headed to the barn.

CJ had unloaded the saddlebags, hung them over a sawhorse, and removed Faith's saddle.

Jillian put her hands on her hips and stretched her lower back. Her muscles ached, especially on the insides of her thighs. "It's been so long since I've been riding that I know I'm going to be sore tomorrow."

He began taking the saddle off Molly. "I had a great time fishing with you today."

"It's been an awesome day." She rested her palm on the Quarter horse's neck. "I'll brush her down if you'll point the way to your supplies."

He gestured in the direction of the back of the barn tack room, and she grabbed what she needed, along with peppermints from a jar. She returned and gave Faith and Molly the treats before brushing down Molly.

CJ carried Faith's saddle and blanket to the tack room, then returned for Molly's saddle and blanket and took those to the room. He came back with another brush to work on the Appaloosa.

Once they finished and had given the pair grain and alfalfa, they headed to the house, throwing a Frisbee for Sadie along the way. CJ stayed out to give the puppy more exercise while Jillian started dinner.

She hummed to herself as she put the glass pan of cornbread mixture into the oven, then coated trout filets to fry. She put the bowl of mixed vegetables she'd brought onto the counter turned on the heat under a steamer with a couple of inches of water, then began frying the fish.

The back door opened and closed, and she looked over her shoulder to see Sadie and CJ. Sadie trotted up and wiggled her butt in excitement, and Jillian took a moment to scratch behind the puppy's ears before returning to frying the trout.

"Everything smells delicious." CJ moved behind her, slid his arms around her, and rested his chin on her shoulder. She shivered inside and reveled in his closeness. He kissed the side of her neck, and she wanted to lean back into him, but she focused on the pan so that she didn't burn herself.

He moved away and put the butter dish on the table for the cornbread and vegetables. He retrieved plates, silverware, and glass tumblers and set the table.

"Iced tea?" he asked.

"Please." She used a pair of tongs to move a fried filet onto a paper towel-covered plate, then set another piece of cornmeal-coated trout into the pan. She set aside the tongs and took a moment to put the vegetables into the steamer, then returned to frying the fish.

It popped and sizzled, and the smell, along with the aroma of baking cornbread, made her stomach growl.

"I heard that—you must be as hungry as I am." He set her iced tea on the counter. "I can take over."

Jillian stepped aside and handed him the tongs. She picked up her glass and sipped from it as she watched the play of muscles in his tanned biceps and forearm as he turned the filet. He was so yummy from head to toe, with his tall, lean, muscled form and the light brown hair that brushed the collar of his T-shirt. He shifted his warm, sable eyes from the pan to her as the timer went off for the cornbread.

She looked down, her cheeks hot from CJ having caught her

watching him. She met his gaze again. "Where are your oven mitts?"

"I'll get it." He set down the tongs on the plate of trout and pulled a couple of hot pads from a drawer. Heat rolled over her when he opened the oven door. He pulled out the pan and set it on the stovetop.

She busied herself, taking the steamer off the stove and pouring out the water before setting the pot on a cool surface of the stovetop.

When everything was done, they filled their plates and settled in at the kitchen table. Sadie crunched puppy food in the corner, where CJ kept her food and water bowls.

He took a forkful of trout, chewed, and swallowed. "Delicious." He made a satisfied sound after eating another bite of fish.

The taste of fresh-caught trout was amazing, and she enjoyed every bite. CJ raved about the cornbread, and he liked the steamed vegetables as well.

They had a pleasant dinner. They never seemed to run out of things to talk about, which made her even more comfortable around him. It was hard to believe they'd been dating for almost three months, yet at the same time, it felt like they'd been together for much longer.

While they talked, she had the feeling that he wanted to tell her something but couldn't get it out. But then it could just have been her imagination.

After they finished dinner, CJ and Jillian cleaned up and loaded the dishwasher. Then, he walked her out to her SUV, Sadie trotting out with them. The stars were brilliant overhead, the only illumination being the floodlight at the kitchen door, some distance away.

Desert temperatures dropped at night unless one lived in Phoenix, where the asphalt, concrete, and glass absorbed the heat and kept everything from warm to hot. King Creek was far enough away from the metro area that it still grew chilly at night. Jillian grabbed her jean jacket off the passenger seat and shrugged it on with CJ's help.

She wished she didn't have to open the store in the morning because she may have ended up staying the night with CJ. She was ready, she just didn't know if he was. He was a man, after all, and every man she had known had been ready to move the relationship forward faster than she'd cared to. Now, was the situation reversed?

CJ raised his head, looked into her eyes, and seemed on the edge of saying something but instead captured her hand. "Goodnight, Jillian. Be careful driving home."

"I will." She smiled as his fingers slipped from hers.

After he opened the driver's side door, he helped her inside and shut the door.

She buzzed down the window. "Goodnight, CJ."

"Get some rest, beautiful." He leaned in and kissed her before stepping away.

She backed up, gave him a little wave, then took off and headed to King Creek.

Memories from the day made her smile all the way home. When she finally climbed into bed, she thought about the kiss and wondered when they would take the next step in their relationship.

11

C J stopped at the gas station to tank up for the trip to Phoenix. He smiled to himself as he pumped the gasoline, thinking about Jillian and his planned day with her.

A red sports car pulled in behind him as he glanced at the fuel dispenser, the numbers whirring by. His vehicle's big tank always took a while to fill, but its mpg wasn't too bad for a truck.

"CJ." A woman's voice caught his attention.

He turned to face the gorgeous blonde. "Hey, Mindy."

She walked over and hugged him, then pulled away and shook her finger. "You haven't called me." She stuck out her lower lip. "I've been dying to get together with you, but I don't have your number."

He never did like to see a grown woman pout or whine.

"Been busy working on the ranch." He glanced at the number of gallons on the display, his tank almost full.

"I heard you're selling your ranch to a corporation," she said.

He almost dropped the nozzle. He shot his gaze back to her. "Where'd you hear that?"

She shrugged. "I have connections, and a good friend mentioned it. The company has big plans, but I didn't get all the details." She tilted her head. "So, it's true?"

CJ clenched his jaw, then forced himself to relax. "I haven't decided."

Mindy moved closer to him and rested her hand on his arm. "Bet you'll be selling it for a pretty penny."

"It's not a done deal." As the lever on the handle clicked and stopped the fuel, he stepped away from her touch. He pulled out the nozzle and put it back in the gasoline dispenser.

She tossed her hair over her shoulder. "Just think what you could do with the money." She waved her hand around them as if to encompass King Creek. "You could get away from this hick town and travel and do whatever you want."

Heat burned the back of his neck. He'd never considered it a hick town, but the rest of her statement hit close to home.

He pulled his keys out of his pocket as he met her gaze. "I haven't made up my mind. Keep this between you and me, please."

Mindy gave him a sly look. "I take it you haven't told Jillian McLeod?"

His scalp prickled. "It's none of your concern, Mindy."

"She'd never leave this place." Mindy leaned up against his truck. "She's got that new store and so many relatives you can't sneeze without bumping into one of them."

"I've got to go." His voice came out tight and controlled.

"Now me, I can't wait to get out of here." She moved closer. "Give me a call, and we can talk it over."

He gripped his door handle, but she was much too close to open the door. "I'll see you around."

She gave her stunning smile, but at that moment, he didn't know what he'd ever seen in her. He'd forgotten just how conniving she was. "Give me your number, and I'll call you when I'm looking at my calendar."

He didn't know how to get his door open without hitting her with it. "Excuse me, Mindy. I've got a date with Jillian, and I'm running behind."

Mindy narrowed her eyes almost imperceptibly. "What do you see in her? She's plain and happy to be stuck here."

Anger weighted CJ's gut like hot lead, but he kept his voice low. "Jillian is one of the most beautiful, kind, caring, and intelligent women that I've ever met." He didn't add "unlike you," but it was probably in his tone.

Mindy's eyes flashed with fire. She knew he'd inferred it and hadn't taken it kindly. She stepped back, her hands clenched at her sides. "You'll regret pushing me away."

She spun and stalked to the sportscar.

CJ closed his eyes a moment and pinched the bridge of his nose. When he opened them again, she backed her car up and zipped to another pump.

He blew out his breath and climbed into his truck, determined to put the woman out of his head. He had more important things to think about, namely the woman he cared about more than anything.

The tension he'd felt from the encounter drained away during the drive, and once again, he was looking forward to spending the day with Jillian.

ON SATURDAY, Jillian had vacillated from the desire to run to the store to ensure everything was running smoothly to being glad to be home and having a day to herself. She hadn't had a pedicure or manicure in ages, and it was the perfect day for both. She also ordered tickets for the *Chicago* musical, which she had access to via an app on her phone.

She did check in at her shop once, but her assistant manager, Kristen, assured her she had everything under control.

That evening, she felt relaxed and rather proud of herself for letting go and allowing herself a day off. She'd had her nails and toenails painted a daring lipstick red. She'd selected a slimming black dress with a princess neckline and red heels for her trip to the musical and dinner with CJ. She picked out yellow gold hoops, a heart necklace, and her gold Movado watch. She had a nice, clear purse with a dainty gold strap, where she could keep her phone, ID, and a small wallet since most venues now required see-through bags and purses.

She wandered into the living room fifteen minutes before CJ was due to arrive. Leeann reclined sideways in an armchair, her legs draped over one arm of the chair, her nose in a book.

On the coffee table sat a short crystal vase with a bright bouquet of star lilies, roses, snapdragons, and sunflowers from her shop. She never tired of beautiful flowers.

Jillian plopped in the chair across from Leeann. "What are you reading?"

Leeann lowered the book to her lap. "It's an assassin novel by David Baldacci. His books are a great way to escape."

"You loaned one to me a year or so ago." Jillian sank into the chair. "I enjoyed it. When I can find the time, I need to start reading more often."

"How are things going with you and CJ?" Leeann shifted in her seat. "Between me working at the hospital and then on my novel in my spare time and you being at work six days a week, we really haven't had time to chat."

"He's everything I ever dreamed of, Leeann." Jillian couldn't help but smile. "I have to pinch myself sometimes because I never thought a guy like him could be interested in me."

"You have got to realize you are beautiful, and you deserve a good man." Leeann shook her head. "You dated that loser far too long—he didn't begin to appreciate you enough."

Jillian waved away the thought of Carl. "He's history." She tried to put into words how CJ made her feel. "CJ is so different. He's loving, caring, considerate, intelligent..."

"All the things the idiot wasn't." Leeann smiled.

"CJ thinks I'm beautiful and tells me that all the time." Jillian nodded slowly. "No one has ever made me feel that way."

With a huff, Leeann swung her legs down and straightened in her chair. She leaned forward. "You *are* beautiful, and we've all told you that."

"You have, and I appreciate it." Jillian brushed a strand of hair out of her eyes. "But you're family, and you love me. What else are you going to say?"

Leeann rolled her eyes to the ceiling. "Heaven, help me." She leaned forward again, her forearms braced on her thighs. "I'm glad CJ is telling you that, and you're listening."

"He's said it enough times that it's starting to stick." Jillian gave a little smile when her sister rolled her eyes again. "But seriously, Leeann, I think he's the *one.*"

"You're in love with him." Leeann sat up straight. "I guessed, but I wasn't sure."

Warmth spread up Jillian's neck. "Yes, head over heels."

"I'm so glad." Leeann grinned. "But if he hurts you, I'm gonna cloud up and rain all over him."

Jillian giggled. "Grandma used to say that when we were kids."

Leeann laughed, too. "I think I'm channeling her. I've never said that before." Then her face turned stern. "But I'm serious. He'd better treat you right and not stomp all over your heart 'cause I'll stomp on him."

With all her heart Jillian hoped that CJ did and would

continue to care for her, but she didn't want to voice that thought aloud.

"I won't be the only one." Leeann brought her knees to her chest and wrapped her arms around them. "Our brothers would probably have a thing or two to say to him."

"I do hope he cares for me like I care for him." Jillian hesitated. "But if he doesn't, I'll move on, and I'll get over it." It would probably take a good long while, but she'd survive.

"You're dressed nicely for a small town." Leeann cocked her head. "What are you doing today?"

Her insides warm, Jillian smiled. "CJ is taking me to Phoenix. We're going to the musical *Chicago* and having dinner at a nice restaurant."

"I adored the movie." Leeann brightened. "I would never have taken CJ for a musical kind of guy."

Jillian shrugged. "He said we could do anything today in the Phoenix area or Tucson, and I told him I'd like to see *Chicago* at the Arizona Broadway Theatre. He didn't bat an eyelash and seemed all for it." She thought about it. "He traveled the world in the Air Force and seems to have enjoyed his travels. He was probably exposed to more in his field than the average cowboy."

"I can see that." Leeann gave a slow nod. "Kit was from L.A. and San Francisco, and she has Carter doing things like that, too. And then there's Tyson and Haylee—they spent a month in Europe."

"Hard to believe our little sister is going to have a Christmas baby." Jillian smiled. "As much of a tomboy as she was, I never really thought about her being a mommy."

"Same here." Leeann shifted her arms around her knees. "What about you? Do you see yourself as a mom?"

Jillian considered the question. "It's never been something I've given too much thought to." She waved her hand in the air. "Considering all of the rugrats in our family, maybe I should have, but it always seemed like more of a *them* thing, not something that I thought about for myself." She leaned back in her chair. "But when Haylee and Tyson made their announcement, it made me think about my future. Yeah, I do think I want kids someday. How about you?"

"I want a big family like we grew up in." Leeann's eyes sparkled.

"Eight kids?" Jillian looked at her, horrified at the thought. "Are you out of your mind?"

Leeann laughed. "Well, maybe not eight, but you never know."

"Can you imagine our family get-togethers?" Jillian shook her head. "There are already too many kids."

"By the time I find someone and settle down, I'll be a full-time novelist." Leeann looked determined. "I have a three-book contract, and my first book is due out around Christmas. I intend to be able to quit my job within two years."

"You can do it." Jillian gave an emphatic nod. "You've always been an amazing writer and have what it takes."

"Thank you." Leeann smiled. "I appreciate that."

A knock at the door startled Jillian and Leeann jumped.

Jillian glanced at her watch. "That's got to be CJ."

She rose from her chair, hurried to the door, and opened it. CJ stood on the other side of the screen door, his sexy smile rocking her world. She pushed open the screen, and he stepped through the doorway. His dark slacks hugged his thighs and his Western dress shirt molded to his chest and biceps.

"Hi, beautiful." CJ brushed his lips over hers, then turned to her sister. "How're you doing today, Leeann?"

She got to her feet. "It's a beautiful day, and I plan to read for hours. So, it'll be perfect." She hugged CJ, surprising Jillian. Although, she shouldn't be surprised since Leeann was a hugger.

CJ reciprocated and smiled as she stepped back. "Glad to hear it."

Leeann slid her hands into her back pockets. "I hear you're going to a musical. Have you gone to many?"

He shrugged one shoulder. "I've been to a few. *Phantom of the Opera* in New York City with my mom years ago, and a couple while I was in the Air Force."

Jillian gave Leeann an "I told you so" look from where she stood, and Leeann smiled impishly back at her.

CJ raised an eyebrow and looked from Leeann to Jillian. "I take it you two don't think cowboys watch musicals."

Jillian raised her hands. "Not me." She nodded in Leeann's direction. "It's that girl."

The corner of CJ's mouth quirked into a grin. "Glad to disabuse you of the notion."

"Let's go." Jillian hitched her purse strap on her shoulder before hugging her sister.

"Have fun." Leeann hugged her back. She turned away and faced CJ. "Take care of my big sister."

"That's my intention." He draped his arm around Jillian's shoulders. "We'll see you later tonight."

"Don't wait up," Jillian shot at Leeann before stepping through the doorway with CJ.

"Oh, I'll want to hear *all* about it," Leeann said before closing the door behind them.

CJ started down the stairs, which squeaked beneath his boot steps. "Do sisters share everything?"

"Absolutely not." Jillian shook her head. "But we do share a lot."

They reached the gate, and CJ held it open for her. "Not having any siblings, I couldn't tell you anything about it."

He helped her into his truck, then climbed into the driver's side. She liked his vehicle's bright, shiny yellow color but preferred her blue SUV for herself.

CJ gripped the steering wheel and looked over at her. "Are you ready for today's adventure?"

She nodded. "I'm excited to go to the musical and glad to see it with you."

"That makes two of us." He started the engine and headed out of her neighborhood.

12

"I haven't been to a musical in ages." Jillian looked over at CJ as they headed north on I-10 for the 2:00 p.m. performance.

"It's probably been even longer for me." He rested his hand on hers on the console, and his touch was warm, strong, and reassuring.

He glanced from the road to her. "How'd you enjoy your day off?"

"It's been wonderful." She let out her breath as he returned his gaze to the freeway. "Thank you for encouraging me to do it."

"You deserve it." He put on his blinker and changed lanes. "But you called in, didn't you."

She eyed him. "Who told you?"

He let out a low laugh. "I guessed. Can't expect you to go cold turkey."

"True." She smiled. "Kristen had everything under control—at least, that's what she led me to believe. But I trust her. She's a great employee and assistant manager."

He was so damned good-looking with his straight nose,

strong jaw, and his bordering-on-too-long hair, that she drank him in.

"Are you planning to hire someone to work for you?" she asked. "You mentioned possibly hiring a 4-H kid."

"I'm to the point of needing to find a little extra help." CJ gave a nod. "I'm going to ask around to find someone with a 4-H contact."

"I'm sure Kaycee can help with that." Jillian pulled her phone out of her purse and typed a message to her niece. "I asked her to text you the number of someone you can get in touch with."

A moment later, Kaycee responded with *Will do.*

Jillian relayed the message to CJ and added, "She's always been a great kid, and now she's a lovely young woman." Jillian sighed. "I can't believe she's almost an adult now."

CJ changed lanes. "I was impressed with Kaycee and Tatum when I met them at your grandpa's birthday party."

"I miss him so much." Jillian looked out the window at the scenery speeding by, struggling to keep from choking up. It had only been a month since he'd passed, and she still got teary thinking about him. "Sometimes I pick up the phone to call Grandpa before I remember he's gone."

CJ put his hand over hers again, giving her strength without saying a word. She faced him. "Thank you for being here for me."

He moved his attention from the freeway to give her a gentle smile. "Of course." He focused on the road again.

She turned her palm up, and he linked his fingers with hers. Her gaze drifted to the eastern sky. "The clouds look dark."

"Weatherman said we'll probably have rain this evening," CJ said.

They arrived at the theatre at 5:00 p.m., close to an hour

before the musical was supposed to start. They walked hand-in-hand along the shaded path to the hall, where they waited for the doors to open so that they could find their seats.

She had purchased the tickets, but only after agreeing with CJ that he would pay for them. They were in the center orchestra section with a great view of the stage.

They settled into their seats, CJ draping his arm around her shoulders. Laughter and chatter surrounded them, making it too loud to speak easily without raising their voices.

An announcement to silence phones reminded her to turn hers off, and then she settled in with anticipation.

The lights dimmed, and CJ moved his arm and took her hand as the production started.

The show was fabulous, and she squeezed his hand tighter during the most exciting points and, at times, had to remind herself to loosen her grip. The musical utterly engrossed her, but she remained keenly aware of the handsome man at her side —the man she had grown to love in such a relatively short time.

Chicago ended far too soon, and she applauded with the crowd, which gave a standing ovation.

CJ leaned close to her ear. "That was one hell of a show."

She flashed him a smile. "I thought you'd enjoy it."

"I sure did." He took her hand again and led her out with the mass of people swirling around them.

They strolled back to the parking garage, Jillian gripping the program in one hand and CJ's hand in her other. Her excitement at seeing the musical bubbled up inside her, and she chatted about it all the way to his truck.

"I'm sorry." She looked up at him as he opened her door. "I've been talking nonstop."

"Don't be." He smiled. "I enjoy listening to you. I had a great time, too."

She took his hand and let him help her into his vehicle.

Once he was in his own seat and had started the engine, he backed up and guided the truck out of the parking garage. Traffic was backed up, so it took a while to make it out.

He pulled the truck onto the street. "I know a great place called King's Fish House, if seafood sounds good to you."

"Oh, yes." She nodded. "I'd love to go there."

"Great." He brought the truck to a stop at a red light. "I've been hankering for a good swordfish steak."

King's wasn't too far, and once he'd parked, he escorted her inside the packed restaurant. She was glad she'd dressed up because it was a nice place.

A hostess seated them at a curved corner booth, and they scooted close to each other. She asked them what drinks they'd like. He ordered a dark beer, and she decided on a Mai Tai.

"There's so much to choose from." She scanned the menu when the hostess left, then looked at CJ. "Do you recommend anything in particular?"

He pointed to the list of specialties. "I've had the grilled Mahi Mahi and the seabass, and both are excellent."

The server showed up and Jillian ordered the Mahi Mahi, and CJ went with his original choice but they decided to forego an appetizer.

When their server retreated, Jillian shifted in her seat so that she could meet his gaze. "I imagine you've had some fabulous seafood in your world travels."

He rested his arm on the back of the seat. "I've had it as often as possible when near an ocean. Most times I love a good rare steak, but seafood is a nice change on occasion.

"I've lived in King Creek my entire life and haven't had the opportunity to travel outside the country." She thought about taking a trip with CJ, and it made her smile. "I'd like the opportunity to visit different places."

He looked intrigued as she said it but just smiled.

The server returned with their drinks and then melted back into the crowded dining room.

"Where have you been to in the world?" she asked.

He named off most European countries, the UK, a few Asian countries, and the southern Pacific.

Her eyes widened. "Holy cow, you've been to a lot of places." She shook her head. "I'm just a small-town girl who wishes to get a chance to see some of the locations you've been to." She settled back in her chair. "But I'm not complaining. I like my life."

"We're both fortunate in how our lives have turned out." He held her gaze. "I feel lucky to have run into you at the state tax office."

"Who would have known a chance encounter would end up where we are." She rested her hand on his thigh. The muscles beneath her palm tightened, and she felt the heat of his flesh through the fabric of his slacks.

He put his hand over hers. "Don't play with fire, beautiful."

She looked into his gorgeous, sable eyes. "I don't mind getting burned."

His expression turned pained, and he shifted in his seat as if his pants were too tight, and she forced herself not to look at his lap. He picked up his beer glass and took a good long swallow.

She sipped her Mai Tai, wondering if she'd been too forward —but they had been dating for almost three months. As far as she was concerned, it wasn't too soon to take the next step.

He cleared his throat. "Have you traveled much in the U.S.?"

She shrugged and moved her hand from his thigh. He seemed to breathe easier when she did. "I've been to several states on girls' trips with my sisters and family vacations."

"Do you have favorite places you've visited?" he asked.

"San Francisco, Boston, and Washington D.C." She wrapped her fingers around her glass, the condensation wetting her fingers. "D.C. is high on my list because of the museums, which I love."

"You'd enjoy Europe." He gave a slow nod. "The cities there are so much older than anything in the U.S., and you find countless museums and places rich with history."

"It's on my bucket list." She sipped the sweet Mai Tai, the tropical flavors rolling over her tongue.

The server showed up with their delicious-smelling entrees and set the plate of grilled Mahi Mahi in front of her and the swordfish before CJ.

When the server left, they resumed talking about their travels as they ate. Jillian felt like a novice compared to CJ, but he seemed interested in her stories of vacations with her family. She, in turn, was enthralled by his travels.

She asked him to tell her about his time in the Air Force as a Pararescue Specialist. He shared some of his experiences, but he wasn't able to go into too much detail due to the nature of his work. What he did tell her was interesting. She couldn't get enough of listening to him.

Dinner had filled her to the brim, so she waved off dessert for herself, and CJ declined as well. The server returned with the check, and CJ gave the young man cash. He bowed and told them to have a good night, then retreated.

Before they got up to leave the booth, CJ paused and gave a soft smile. "Have I told you how beautiful you look tonight, Jillian?"

Heat rose to her cheeks. "Thank you."

He leaned forward and brushed his lips over hers, and she had to fight to not moan with all the need pent up inside her.

When he drew away, he seemed to drink her in. "I wish the night wasn't ending so soon."

She tore her gaze from his and looked at her watch before meeting his eyes again. "It's not too late. Why don't we go to your ranch before you take me home? I haven't seen Sadie for a whole week."

He studied her, and heat crept up her neck. She bit her lower lip—she had to be so transparent that he could see how much she wanted him.

"I'm sure she'll be happy to see you." He slid out of the booth, and she scooted over to her side. He came over to her, held out his hand, helping her to her feet.

Her heart pounded a little faster, and her belly fluttered as they walked out to his truck. When they were both seated inside, he paused a moment, like he was debating with himself, and then his expression turned resolved.

"I need to talk with you," he said. "My place is better than here, in my truck."

She wrinkled her forehead, not sure what he was saying. "All right," she said slowly. "We can talk."

At first, they were quiet on the way to his ranch. But then he started asking her about trips she'd taken with her family again, and she was happy to continue the discussion. He did seem keen on knowing how she felt about it.

As they drove, lightning flashes lit up the sky in the direction of the Superstition Mountains and King Creek.

After parking and going into the house, the first thing CJ did was let Sadie out of her kennel. She jumped and barked and wiggled her butt with excitement. Jillian hugged the puppy and then they took the Aussie outside to relieve herself, and CJ played a bit of tug-of-war with her.

It started to sprinkle, and lightning lit up the night.

"We'd better get in." CJ gave Sadie a hand signal to return to the house.

When they went back in, CJ produced a bottle of wine and poured her a glass, then grabbed a beer for himself. After making sure Sadie had plenty of food and clean water, they went to his comfy back room and seated themselves on the couch, their thighs pressed against each other.

Rain began pounding against the window, and a flash of lightning was followed by the crack of thunder. It felt cozy in the room with CJ, hidden away from the storm.

Jillian took a long sip of wine, the alcohol warming her chest. She set the glass on the coffee table and eased closer to him, their knees touching. He set his beer down, and she leaned in for a kiss.

He lowered his head and moved his mouth over hers. His lips felt so firm, and his kiss heated her through. He slid his tongue into her mouth, and she sighed with pleasure. The taste of him, the scent of him—she loved everything about him.

With a groan, he brought her onto his lap, and she slid her arms around his neck. Their kiss grew more passionate, and desire flooded her body. He slid his hand over her breast and teased her nipple with his fingers, and sensation flared through her body. She wriggled, arching her body into his touch. The feel of his hard cock against her buttocks fueled the fire.

CJ groaned again and drew back. He put his forehead against hers, his breathing heavy. "We have to stop."

Jillian's mind was hazed with her arousal, and she had to pull herself together to process what he was saying.

She managed to get one word out. "Why?"

"We need to talk first." He raised his head and met her gaze. "I have something to tell you."

The back of her neck prickled with a warning. What could he have to say that was so important?

He eased her onto the couch and shifted her so that they were facing each other, their knees touching. He looked so serious that her belly twisted.

She swallowed down the rush of fear that threatened to engulf her. "What is it?"

He closed his eyes a moment before opening them. "You mean the world to me, Jillian."

She held her breath. It wasn't an *"I love you,"* but it was a step closer.

Yet, she sensed a "but" coming.

He held her gaze. "I'm selling the ranch, and I plan to travel the world."

She reeled back, not quite comprehending what he was saying.

"The corporation that offered to buy my place when I inherited it is paying me more money than I could use in a lifetime." His throat worked as he swallowed. "I want you to go with me." He waited for her to respond, but she couldn't speak. "Please."

Prickles ran along her flesh. "I—" She shook her head. "I have my family and my business, something I've always dreamed of. I can't just take off."

A disappointed expression crossed his strong features. "Think about it."

"No." Her tone was resolute. "I'd also like to start a family. I can't do that while jaunting all over the place."

He studied her for a long moment before he asked again, "Please, just think about it."

She ignored his request. "What are you going to do with Sadie?"

"Take her with me." CJ continued to hold Jillian's gaze. "By the time the place is ready, and the contract signed, she'll be old enough and well-trained. I'd really like you to go with us."

Jillian bit her lower lip. She loved him enough that she could imagine going with him and Sadie. But this was her home, and she had plans and dreams of her own.

And he just cared for her. He hadn't even said he loved her.

"I'm ready to go home." Jillian got to her feet.

"I'm sorry." He stood and took her hands. "I should have told you sooner, but I hadn't made up my mind until yesterday."

"Yes, you should have told me." Tears pricked at the backs of her eyes, but she wasn't going to cry. She pulled her hands away and walked to the kitchen.

Sadie trotted at her side, and CJ followed. She took her purse off the kitchen table, where she'd left it, and held it tightly to her chest.

He had a regretful expression in his gaze, but he couldn't have more regrets than she had. She'd given her heart to this man, and he was walking away from her. *He* had made that decision without telling her that it was a possibility. If she'd known from the beginning, she wouldn't be torn up inside like she was now.

Jillian knelt and gave Sadie a big hug and almost lost it. It was probably the last time she would ever see the puppy. She pulled herself together and waited for CJ to put the Aussie into the kennel.

They walked out to the truck, rain pouring down. She blinked against the rain rolling over her face and into her eyes. Lightning lit up the land, followed by thunder. By the time they got to the vehicle, she was soaked through.

It wasn't long before they were on their way to King Creek.

Silence reigned on the drive back. Either CJ didn't know what to say, or he realized Jillian didn't want to talk—maybe both.

When they were parked, rain thrummed on the truck's roof. She didn't want to wait for him to help her get out, but he was around the truck before she could climb down, and he took her hand. She pulled it away as soon as she was on her feet.

She stood and met his gaze. "I can walk to the door myself."

He looked desperate to get her to talk to him. "Jillian, I don't like leaving things like this between us."

"There's nothing to say." She forced herself to respond calmly. "You've made what you believe is the right decision for you. I've told you my decision. I wish you the best of luck."

She turned before he could say anything else, her back straight and her chin high as she strode along the sidewalk, through the rain, and up the steps. She never looked back as she walked or when she used the key to open the door. The latch clicked into place behind her before the first teardrop rolled down her cheek, mingling with the raindrops wetting her face.

"Jill, honey, what's wrong?" Leeann's concerned voice came from the direction of the hallway.

Jillian waved her hand like she was brushing off her sister's concern. "I'll be fine."

"Sit." Leeann pointed to Jillian's favorite chair. "I can see we need to talk."

Knowing it was pointless to argue, she took her seat. "I really don't want to."

Leeann plopped into the armchair across from her. "Too bad." She set her jaw. "I need to kill him, don't I."

Jillian almost smiled. Instead, she pushed wet hair out of her face as she shook her head. "CJ is selling the ranch for a sum that will set him up for life. When he does, he's leaving to travel the world."

Leeann's jaw dropped. "And he's just telling you this *now*?"

"Yes." Jillian gripped her fingers in her lap. "He asked me to go with him and Sadie. He said I mean the world to him."

"What did you say?" Leeann asked quietly.

"I have a life here." Jillian looked at her sister. "I have a new business that's been my dream for as long as I can remember. All my family is here, and someday, I'd like to have children of my own. This is my home."

Leeann slowly nodded. "What was his reply?"

"He asked me to please think about it." Jillian shook her

head. "What's there to think about? I gave him my response, and there's no changing my mind."

"And he's just now getting around to telling you." Leeann narrowed her gaze.

Jillian let out a long breath. "He said he hadn't made up his mind until yesterday."

"That's no excuse." Leeann's expression hardened. "He should have told you that the minute he considered selling it."

"He said they made the offer when he inherited the property." Jillian put her fingertips to her forehead. "That means he knew about this when we first met, yet he never mentioned it."

"That's it." Leeann's voice cut the air. "I'm killing him first thing in the morning."

"You have to work." Jillian lowered her hands and did manage a smile, but it faded. "He's made his choice, Leeann. What's done is done."

"I'll take the day off."

"I'll be okay." Jillian struggled not to cry, but another tear escaped and rolled down her cheek. "I told you earlier that I'd move on if something happened between us. That's exactly what I'm going to do."

"Oh, sweetie." Kneeling in front of Jillian, Leeann wrapped her arms around Jillian and hugged her. "I'm so sorry."

Jillian leaned into her sister's hug, and more tears rolled down her cheeks. She was so glad she hadn't cried in front of CJ. That would have made the whole situation even worse.

Leeann held her for a long moment before drawing away. She reached for a tissue from the box on the end table and handed it to Jillian.

She took the Kleenex and dabbed at her eyes before blowing her nose, then crumpled the tissue in her hand. "Monday morning, I'll go to work and keep busy. It might take me a couple of days to get used to the idea that he's gone from my life, but that's what I'm going to do."

"You're stronger than I am." Leeann squeezed Jillian's forearm. "You always have been."

Jillian gave a sad smile. "We're both stronger than we think." She stood, and Leeann joined her. "I'm going to bed now. Everything will look brighter in the morning."

She hoped.

C J sat behind his desk in front of his laptop the Monday morning following his talk with Jillian. His gut ached at the thought of never seeing her again, never spending Sundays with her, or calling her during the week. How would he handle running into her in town?

He planned to tour the world, and there was a good chance he and Sadie wouldn't come back. If he didn't have Jillian, there would be nothing to come back to.

His phone lay on his desk in front of him, and he stared at it. Something ate at the back of his brain, along with what was eating at his heart. He picked up the phone, found Jim Butcher's number, pressed the connect icon, and put the phone on speaker.

"CJ," came Butcher's jovial voice after a couple of rings. "How's things with our ranch?"

"I'd like to visit one of your other dude ranches." CJ leaned back in his chair. "I want to get an idea of what you'll be doing with my place."

Butcher hesitated only a moment. "By all means. We have a

couple in California, one in Texas, and another in New Mexico. Which one would you like to visit?"

"New Mexico sounds good." That location would be more like his property than something in California. "Give me the details."

"It's called Lone Pine Mesa." Butcher muffled the phone and coughed before continuing. "We'll fly you out there on our dime."

"I've got it." CJ typed "Lone Pine Mesa New Mexico Dude Ranch" into the bar on the search engine. A website for the ranch popped up, and he clicked the Directions tab. "I'll fly to New Mexico this afternoon, find a place to hole up, and be there first thing in the morning."

"You're welcome to stay the night at the ranch," Butcher said. "You'll have a better idea of what we do—tell Greta I sent you. I'll contact her as soon as we hang up."

"I'll take you up on that." CJ did like the idea of a more personal experience since that was what his property would become once the corporation took over his place.

Butcher sounded cautious as he asked, "Why so soon?"

"Why not?" CJ pulled up Southwest Airlines in another tab. "I'll talk with you tomorrow."

He disconnected, found a direct flight to Albuquerque, leaving at 1:05 p.m., and booked it. He scheduled a rental car for the three-hour drive from the airport to the dude ranch.

Bear McLeod's cell number was in his contacts, and he wondered if his veterinary practice had pet boarding. He called, and Bear answered, told CJ they did, and gave him the number for the front office.

It wasn't much longer before he had arranged a time to drop Sadie off. He'd feed his livestock before leaving. He'd be back late tomorrow afternoon—everything would be fine until he returned.

. . .

CJ's FLIGHT landed in Albuquerque at 2:15 p.m. By the time he got the rental car and drove to Lone Pine Mesa Dude Ranch, it was almost 6:00 p.m. He was glad he was staying there since he wouldn't have a lot of time before he had to drive back to Albuquerque. He'd have to leave by 1:00 p.m. tomorrow to make his flight.

The entire day he'd thought of Jillian, his chest feeling like an anvil pressed down on him. How could he leave her behind?

The rustic main house made of split logs was lit up on his arrival, the yellow glow spilling from the windows. The cool forest air made him glad he'd opted for a light jacket. The air smelled fresh, of pine and rich earth.

Cattle lowed from a corral to the east as he walked from the dusty parking lot to the front porch. In the distance, the sounds of conversation and laughter met his ears. It appeared to come from around the corner on the west side of the main house.

Inside, a chandelier made of elk antlers hung from the open-beamed ceiling. Southwestern rugs lay beneath heavy pine furniture. Oil paintings depicting cowboys on horseback driving cattle, some riding into the sunset, while others sat around a campfire, and more hung from the walls.

A woman decked in a plaid shirt manned the registration desk, *Greta* on her nametag.

The redheaded older woman smiled at him. "Howdy. How may I help you?"

"Ma'am." CJ touched the brim of his hat. "I'm CJ Jameson. Jim Butcher said he'd let you know I was coming in from Arizona."

"Yes." She turned a big, hard-bound book around, opened it, and held out a pen. "Please sign our guestbook, and I'll get your key."

CJ took the pen and scrawled his signature on a line beneath other names in the book. Greta asked him for his ID and checked him in on a computer.

She handed him an old-fashioned key. "You'll be staying here in the main house rather than one of the cabins around the property." She nodded in the direction of the stairs. "Your room is on the second floor, to the right, room number 23."

He took the key. "Thank you kindly, ma'am." He headed to the right and up the stairs to his room.

The simple and small space had a queen-sized bed, oak furnishings, and a painting depicting a rider on horseback at a creek on one wall. After CJ left his duffel bag on the bed, he headed back downstairs, his stomach growling.

When he walked into the empty reception area, he spotted Greta. "Is there a place where I can get a bite?" he asked.

She nodded. "Yes, but tonight we're having a campfire cook-out. It's getting started now. Just head on out to your left—you can't miss it." She handed him a sheet of paper. "Tomorrow's activities. Too bad you won't be here for the evening barn dance."

CJ thanked her, folded the paper, and put it into his back pocket, then walked out into the cool evening in her indicated direction. A dark, star-strewn sky reminded him of nights at home. Only in the Arizona desert, it stretched for miles instead of just visible where there were no trees.

A bonfire blazed and crackled, its yellow and orange flames dancing and reflecting on the faces of several men and a few women, who relaxed in canvas chairs. Most had plates filled with food from a long table on the other side of the fire. Smells of woodsmoke and grilled meats filled the air.

After sweeping his gaze around the circle, CJ went to the chow table. A server in a cowgirl outfit handed CJ an empty plate.

"Enjoy your supper," the woman said in a thick country drawl that didn't sound authentic to CJ's ear.

He filled his plate with a cowboy steak, baked potato, cornbread, and pinto beans. He then sat between a burly man with some bulk on him and another gentleman, with half the width and a good deal shorter.

CJ introduced himself to the smaller man, who shook CJ's hand and told him that his name was Trevor.

After accepting a beer from a woman in a cowgirl shirt and tight jeans, CJ turned to the man. "Are you enjoying yourself, Trevor?"

The man, who wore fancy dude duds, nodded. "I've always wanted to live like a cowboy."

CJ had his doubts that Trevor would enjoy a real cowboy's lifestyle. "How long have you been here?"

"Just arrived this afternoon." The man held a fork and looked at the plate in his lap. "This looks good."

The meal was decent, and CJ listened to Trevor's excited babble as he ate.

CJ turned to the big man on his left, and they made introductions. The man's name was Phil. CJ asked him the same questions he'd asked Trevor.

"Okay, so far," Phil muttered. "Got in last night."

CJ spent most of the time around the fire, listening and observing. He tried to picture the same scene at his own ranch and had a hard time doing so. How would his neighbors feel about having a bunch of city slickers playing cowboy nearby? He thought again about his parents, who had loved the land despite having rough years. It was often feast or famine.

After dinner, CJ went into the saloon in the right wing of the sprawling main house. A bartender poured him a whiskey straight, and he leaned up against a support beam as he watched a group of men play poker. The dealer wore an Old West gambler's outfit and talked in a drawl as exaggerated as most of the other employees he'd heard speaking.

CJ observed other men and women in the saloon, who seemed to be enjoying themselves for the most part. Most looked like they worked someplace like Wall Street but dressed in urban cowboy garb.

Even though he was trying to focus on his surroundings and the folks in it, his attention kept drifting back to Jillian and the betrayal he'd seen in her eyes. He hadn't meant to hurt her, but what had he been thinking? He'd led her to believe they had the possibility of a future together. Only he'd hoped she'd say yes to coming with him.

He hadn't just hurt her—the pain he felt was like a knife to his own heart. Every memory that came to mind twisted the blade even deeper. Her sweetness, beauty, intelligence, and caring—how could he ever meet another woman who made him feel as alive as she had?

To get his mind off the ache in his chest, he joined a table of men playing Texas Hold 'em. He held his own and ended up winning a good number of poker chips. Gambling, including poker, was illegal in New Mexico, everywhere but on the reservations. So, the poker chips could only be traded for snacks and drinks at the bar.

When it grew late, CJ headed up to his room. If he and Jillian had still been dating, he would have called her and shared his day's experiences. The fact that he couldn't talk with her about it made him feel hollow inside.

THE NEXT MORNING, CJ woke still thinking about Jillian. He tried to push thoughts of her aside as he headed downstairs at 6:30 a.m., but he had a hell of a hard time doing so.

He talked with Greta at the registration desk, and she told

him breakfast was any time before 9:00 a.m. in the chow hall, and lunch started at 11:00 a.m.

People came in and out of the hall as CJ sat between a gentleman named Henry, and a woman, Carrie. He quizzed them both on how they were enjoying the dude ranch and what they'd done so far. They both seemed to have had positive experiences.

After breakfast, CJ sauntered out to the corral, where a cowboy was giving roping lessons to a group of city slickers. He watched several of the guests attempt to lasso a steer dummy, none of them having much success. The cowboy asked CJ if he'd like to give it a try, but he declined. He'd learned how to lasso at the age of four, so he'd just be showing off, and he was here to observe.

In another corral, a cowgirl instructed guests on how to ride a horse. After they mounted on a gentle mare, she let them ride around the corral to get used to being in the saddle.

"You'll have the opportunity to go for a ride later this afternoon," the cowgirl said. "First, you need to learn the basics." She smiled. "At the end of the day, you'll find yourself saddle-sore."

Since he'd grown up on the back of a horse, CJ didn't know what it was like to be good and sore from a horse ride. However, due to being away while in the service, or if it had been a long time between times astride one of the big animals, he'd find his legs would have a bit of an ache at the end of a long ride, but not much.

He pulled the list of activities out of his back pocket and scanned it. Earlier that morning had been a sunrise ride for those with at least basic training.

Some with more experience were invited to join a cattle drive as long as they signed a waiver beforehand. Others could participate in sorting and pairing.

Additional activities guests could enjoy included swimming

and fishing in a nearby lake, hiking, rock climbing, and mountain biking in the wilderness, archery and shooting sports, gold-
panning, bird-watching, and riding ATVs or UTVs.

At noon, CJ headed for the chow hall to get a bite to eat
before leaving for the airport. He continued to churn in his
mind what he'd seen and learned about dude ranches as he
drove from Lone Pine Mesa to Albuquerque and on his flight
back.

He tried to picture those activities on his own place and all
the people coming and going. Would the dude ranch have a
negative effect on property values around King Creek? What
kind of impact would it make on local wildlife? The small lake
he and Jillian had fished at would be over-fished, become
polluted, with garbage scattered around the shore.

Was he doing a disservice to those around him in other
ways?

Would he be benefiting to the detriment of the people and
the land?

When he got back to King Creek, he picked up Sadie and
headed home. He fed the livestock, then went into his house, the
Aussie bounding along beside him.

He had a lot to think about. He wished he could call Jillian
and get her input, but he had to figure out this for himself.

A LUMP HAD BEEN CROWDING Jillian's throat all day. She refused
to cry, but her eyes still ached from the hole CJ had left in her
heart. It was Wednesday, four days after he told her that he
would be leaving.

She wiped a clean cloth over the glass countertop and
stopped to rub off a sticky spot.

Maybe in the past, she would have cried her eyes out, but she
was stronger now and she would survive and hopefully love

again. But it would be a while before her heart could fully heal and she wouldn't be afraid to give it to another man.

Her sisters had been supportive and wanted to castrate CJ. It did make her smile a little, but she'd insisted she was fine and would move on.

Easier said than done.

She sprayed 409 on the sticky spot, and it finally wiped clean. The bells on the front door jangled, and she looked up. Her heart stuttered.

CJ strode toward her, a cautious smile on his features.

She couldn't return the smile, so she waited for him to reach her.

"Hi, Jillian." The low timbre of his voice caused a flutter in her belly. She'd always loved how he said her name. "How are you?"

"Fine." She swallowed. "Is there something I can do for you?"

He looked pained at her terse response. "Can we talk? Is it possible for you to get away?"

She shook her head. "I'm busy, and there's no one here to cover me anyway."

He rested his hands on the countertop. "I'm sorry for the way I've handled things."

She shrugged and set the cleaning cloth and 409 aside. "You didn't need to come here to tell me that."

"That's not why I'm here." He took her hands in his, catching her off guard. He raised them and put her palms against his chest. "I'm here because I can't live without you."

She tried to pull away. "And I can't go with you. There's no sense in rehashing this."

He didn't let go and held her gaze. "I love you, Jillian."

Her eyes widened, and tingles raced over her skin. She didn't trust herself not to say something stupid, so she remained quiet.

He squeezed her hands tighter to his chest. "I would do anything for you, and that includes staying here."

She caught her breath. "You're not leaving?"

He gave her a tentative smile. "I'm not going anywhere, and I've decided not to sell the ranch. I think it would be a great place to raise a passel of kids. Being with you and our children would make me happier than traveling anywhere in the world alone."

Her heart rate sped up, and she bit her lower lip, hardly able to believe her ears. He loved her, and he was staying in King Creek.

He released her hands. "Will you come on this side of the counter so I can do this right?"

Like a sleepwalker, she obeyed him. When she stood in front of him, he slipped a small box from his pocket and opened it. Inside the black box, nestled in black velvet, was a two-carat diamond solitaire.

Blood rushed in her ears as she stared at it, mesmerized and unable to believe what she was seeing.

He set the box on the counter, took the ring and her left hand. "Jillian, will you marry me?"

She clapped her free hand over her mouth before she lowered it. She looked from the hypnotic sparkle of the ring to meet his eyes. "I love you, CJ." Her heart beat a hundred miles a minute as his face broke into a grin. "Yes. *Yes*, I will marry you."

He slid the ring on her finger then whooped, picked her up, and swung her around. He crushed her to him and then set her on her feet. He cupped her face in his hands and lowered his mouth to hers.

Their kiss was long and fierce, filled with the passion of their love. She breathed in his familiar scent that she'd missed, felt the strength of his arms, and savored the taste of him.

When they parted, she looked into his eyes and saw the depth of his care for her.

"I don't know whether to string you up, CJ, or welcome you to the family," Leeann said from behind them.

CJ draped his arm around Jillian's shoulders as they turned to face Leeann, who had her arms folded across her chest, an appraising light to her eyes.

"I deserve the stringing up," CJ said, "but I'm hoping for the welcome."

Leeann studied him with a hard expression, which melted into a grin. "Welcome to the family." She rushed forward and hugged Jillian's future husband, then flung her arms around Jillian and hugged her, too.

When Leeann stepped back, she said, "So when's the wedding?"

Jillian looked at the ring. "I'm still trying to get used to this whole getting married thing."

CJ met Jillian's gaze. "The sooner the better."

Leeann leaned against the counter. "Looks like I am now the only single McLeod sibling." She waved toward the door. "Go on now and celebrate. I'll take over."

"Thank you, sis." Jillian headed toward the back room. "Give me a minute to grab my purse, CJ."

Moments later, CJ and Jillian walked out to his truck. Once they were both inside, CJ looked at her. "I can take you out for dinner, or we can pick something up to take to my place."

"Let's pick something up." She took his hand on the console. "It'll be nice to be alone for the evening and spend time with our kids' future protector."

"Sadie will be great at that." CJ flashed her a grin. "How many rugrats do you want?"

She sank back against her seat. "Two or three, eventually."

He squeezed her hand. "We can start at two and work our way up."

She studied CJ's handsome profile and smiled. "Deal."

After a moment, she said, "What made you decide not to sell? You would have been set for life and could have found another place to live in King Creek."

He shrugged one big shoulder. "I grew up on this ranch, and I think it's a good place for a family. Our family." He glanced at her before looking back at the road. "I visited a dude ranch in New Mexico—went on Monday and came home yesterday. After spending a little time there, it just didn't feel right to sell to a big corporation that would bring in thousands of people from all over, increase traffic and pollution, and damage the land."

"I'm sure everyone around here would be grateful to know that you made that choice," Jillian said. "I am. It would be hard to see any of that happening."

"What are you hungry for?" he asked.

She pointed up ahead at Ricardo's. "How about Mexican food?"

"Sounds great to me."

Jillian smiled to herself. Anything sounded good as long as she was with the man she was going to spend the rest of her life with.

CJ carried the bags into the house, and Jillian let Sadie out of her kennel. The puppy pranced and bumped her head against Jillian's hand, asking for attention. She took the Aussie out so the dog could pee and stretch her legs.

After Sadie was fed and watered, Jillian and CJ sat at the kitchen table to eat across from each other. Her diamond glittered in the light, and she smiled at the man she loved. It didn't take long to eat and clean up.

CJ took her hands in his and pressed his body against hers. He kissed her, so long and sweet it stole her breath.

Desire stirred within her, and she could feel the hard ridge of his own need against her belly.

When they parted, he took her hand and led her down the hallway to his room. Her heart thundered, and her belly quivered.

He stopped at the foot of his bed and met her gaze as he brushed a lock of hair from her cheek. "I've been wanting this with you for a long time."

"I have, too." Her words came out low and filled with pent-up desire.

He kissed her with a hunger that nearly made her knees give out on her. She pressed herself against him, needing him more than she'd ever needed anything in her life.

CJ broke the kiss and fumbled with the top button of Jillian's blouse, then worked his way down. He pushed it over her shoulders, and she let it slide to the floor. Her nipples were hard peaks, pushing against her bra cup. He reached around her and unfastened it, and it followed the same path as the other garment.

Her heart pounded faster as he cupped her breasts and rubbed his thumbs over her sensitive nubs. A moan rose within her, and she shuddered from his touch. He lowered his head and slipped her nipple into his mouth.

She gasped and gripped his shoulders so tightly her knuckles ached as he licked and sucked first one, then the other. She trembled and whimpered at the feel of it.

He knelt in front of her and pressed kisses to her belly. He took one of her feet, slid the ballet flat off, and tossed it aside before doing the same with her other shoe. The tile floor felt cool beneath her bare feet.

CJ moved his fingers to the button on her slacks and slid it through its hole. Her nipples, still damp from his mouth, puckered tighter. He pushed the slacks and her panties over her hips to her feet and held her hand as she stepped out of them. Those articles of clothing went the same way her shoes had.

She stood naked before him, still trembling, as he rose to his feet. He swept his gaze over her from head to toe before meeting her eyes. "You are so beautiful, Jillian. Everything about you is, from your big heart to your intelligence to your gorgeous body."

Heat rushed through her at the way he said it—they weren't just words, but something he truly meant and felt.

"It's your turn." She reached for his shirt and began unbuttoning it, her hands shaking.

He undid his belt buckle and pulled the belt from its loops as she tackled his shirt. The buckle hit the floor with a hard thump. He shrugged out of his shirt and tossed it aside.

"Let's get those boots off." Jillian pushed him back against the bed, and he dropped to the mattress, grinning.

He toed off one boot, and she helped him pull off the other. They made hard thunks when they hit the floor. She peeled off each of his socks, dropping them. He leaned back, his hands braced on the quilt as she unfastened and unzipped his Wranglers.

Her breathing grew heavy with anticipation as he assisted her in shucking off the jeans. His boxer briefs remained, his rigid cock pressing against the stretchy fabric. She hooked her fingers in the sides of the boxers and tugged them down to his feet, and he kicked them away.

She pushed between his thighs and wrapped her fingers around his length, and he sucked air through his teeth. His cock felt like silk-covered steel beneath her palm.

Jillian rubbed her thumb over the head through a drop of his fluid. She lowered her head and slipped him into her mouth. He groaned and slid his fingers into her hair. She looked up at him as her mouth traveled up and down his length, and his eyes reflected his pain in holding back his release.

She sucked and licked him, and he clenched her head in his palms. She loved that he seemed so close to losing control. She stopped long enough to say, "Do it. I want to taste you," before she sucked him again.

His hoarse shout cut the air as his hips bucked, and he filled her mouth with his fluid. She continued to apply suction as she swallowed every bit.

"Stop, Jillian." He groaned again. "No more. I can't take it."

She let him slide from her mouth and smiled up at him. "That was fun."

He gave a low, pained chuckle. "I like your idea of fun."

She squealed with laughter as he picked her up and twisted to drop her onto the mattress. He knelt on the floor, grasped her knees, and dragged her close to the edge. "Now I'm gonna get even."

Her giggles died in her throat as his big shoulders spread her thighs apart, and he buried his face against her center.

Sheer pleasure engulfed her. He ran his tongue along her slick flesh, then concentrated on the sensitive nub, causing her to writhe beneath him.

The incredible sensations whirled inside her and carried her away to the precipice of an orgasm. He sucked, and she lost it. She screamed, thrill after thrill rolling through her. She squirmed as he erotically tortured her much the same as she had tortured him.

"That's enough." She had a hard time catching her breath, and her words echoed his earlier ones. "*Please* stop, CJ. I can't take any more."

He raised his head and grinned at her. "Fair is fair." He didn't give her a chance to respond and picked her up and moved her to the center of the bed.

His gaze softened. "How soon do you want kids."

She caught her breath, surprised at his words. "Depends. When are we getting married?"

He nuzzled her ear. "How does tomorrow sound?"

She laughed. "Let's give it a week." She pressed her palm against his cheek. "As far as wanting kids, I'm ready when you are."

"Then how about we start now." He placed the head of his erection against her center, waiting for her response.

She nodded. "Yes, now."

CJ slid inside her, stretching her. Jillian's eyes widened as he filled her completely. He began sliding in and out at a slow, steady pace. She arched her hips, pressing herself against him, then moved in tandem with his strokes.

It felt so good having him inside her, this man she loved with everything she had. The heady knowledge that they would soon marry and start a family filled her heart and made the experience mean even more.

He thrust hard, and his rhythm increased. She matched his urgency, the need for completion with him inside her, making her feel whole.

A fine sheen of perspiration coated their skin, and a flush of heat stole through her as they charged closer to orgasm. Harder, faster, and more intense with every moment.

She could barely think past the pleasure and nearly lost it. She held back, wanting to climax when he did.

"Are you ready, beautiful?" His words came out strong but filled with the tension coiling in his body.

"Yes." She nodded, her hair sliding on the quilt.

"Come now, Jillian," he shouted. "Come *now*."

She shrieked with the orgasm that slammed into her, and he shouted his own release. They moved together, drawing out their orgasms. Her core clenched down on his cock as it throbbed inside her.

They stopped, both of them breathing hard. He rolled onto his side and brought her with him so that they were facing each other, their legs intertwined.

He stroked damp hair from her forehead and smiled. "My beautiful love."

She rested her left hand on his hip, the diamond sparkling on her finger. She smiled. "My handsome man, whom I love with all my heart."

He returned her smile and sealed the moment with a kiss.

. . .

JILLIAN SAT across from CJ in front of the small bakery in Bath, England. They had spent the day at Stonehenge and had explored Windsor Castle, and now they were enjoying a relaxing English tea.

After a whirlwind wedding in Las Vegas with all her family in attendance, CJ had whisked her off to Western Europe, and sadly, their trip was almost to an end.

She broke off a piece of the scone on her plate, slathered on clotted cream, then spread strawberry jam on top of that. She took a bite and enjoyed the smooth thickness of the cream and the sweetness of the jam.

CJ watched her with amusement as she sighed with pleasure. "When we get back to the U.S., I'm going to miss tea and scones," she said.

He swept his gaze over the square in Bath City Centre, the people walking from shop to shop on the pavers, and the imposing church on the opposite end. He met Jillian's eyes. "I'm going to miss having all this time with you to myself." He leaned closer. "A month hasn't been nearly enough. What do you say about spending another week in this part of the world? We could go to Vienna or Prague next. I know you'll love either one."

"As long as I'm with you, I'll enjoy any place in the world." She broke off another piece of scone. "But don't tempt me. I need to get back to my store—my sisters have been holding down the fort, but I shouldn't be away too long."

He watched her add the clotted cream and jam to the piece on her plate. "Haylee and Leeann wouldn't mind."

Jillian picked up her teacup of Lady Grey tea with milk. "You're right, but that doesn't mean I should stay away."

He smiled. "Am I at least tempting you?"

She sipped her tea, then set the cup on its saucer with a light clink. It was her turn to look amused. "Yes, but we should probably go home."

"Aha." He leaned back in his seat. "You said *probably*. That means there's a chance you'll say yes."

She laughed. "I need to bring in more revenue so that we can enjoy more of these trips."

He smiled. "The ranch will be up to full speed soon and start turning a profit, and I have plenty saved up from my time in the service that we can take an annual trip."

"Ah, but we're working on a family." She gave him a mischievous smile. "Kids equals more money. *Lots.* Believe me, I've heard about it from all my siblings, save Leeann." She tipped her head to the side. "Even Haylee has talked about the expense of preparing for a child, and their baby isn't due for another two months."

He looked amused again. "We'll do just fine, beautiful."

Her heart burst with love. This wonderful man had come into her life and would do anything for her, and she would do the same for him. She'd never dreamed she could be this happy.

They chatted about their day at Stonehenge and Windsor Castle. They had plans to go to an authentic English Pub in Lacock, near Cotswold, on the way back to London. Jillian was anxious to see the place where scenes from the Harry Potter movies and Downton Abbey had been filmed.

"Our kids will learn all about the magic of Harry Potter," she said as they strolled through the Centre.

CJ grinned. "And the One Ring, the Force, and travels to where no one has gone before."

"Yep." She peeked through the windows of a glass-makers shop. "Let's go in here. I bet we'll find something handblown for our future ornament tree." They had purchased ornaments from every location they'd visited in Europe and had decided to buy a

small tree to put them on in addition to their regular tree and
have both up at Christmastime.

They explored the small shop, and Jillian loved all the handblown items that had been created. She and CJ picked out a
heart ornament with a colorful design.

Next, they went to an antique market, a shopping arcade,
and a silver jewelry store, where CJ bought her a charm bracelet.
He had been spoiling her with jewelry the entire trip.

As the day wound down, they decided to head to Lacock for
dinner. CJ was adept at driving on the left side of the road, so
they had rented a car.

They walked hand-in-hand to the parked vehicle, and she
looked up at CJ. "You know what?" she said.

He looked down at her. "Yes?"

"I've decided I don't want our time here to end." She beamed
at him. "I'll call Leeann and see if they can watch the shop for
another week."

His face split into a grin. "I'll get ahold of the foreman I just
hired to make sure he can go another week alone. I don't think
that will be a problem."

"Good." She swung hands with him. "I hear Prague is
gorgeous."

He nodded. "It's one of my favorite places in Europe."

"Let's go there next." Jillian leaned into him. "Being honest,
though, any place with you is my favorite place."

CJ put his arm around her shoulders. "Honey, that makes
two of us."

EXCERPT: COUNTRY FROST

Coming Winter 2024

1

———

Leeann McLeod leaned back against the corral and rested her arms on the rail as she watched the truck coming up the drive to Carter's home, a cloud of dust roiling behind it.

"That must be the farrier." Leeann glanced at her brother. "Have you met him?"

"Nah." Carter shook his head. "Tyson recommended the guy since old man Winters retired."

Her gaze followed the black Ford as it pulled up to the barn and stopped. "If our brother-in-law recommended him, he's got to be good."

"Yep." Carter headed toward the truck, which had a shell with double doors in the back instead of a tailgate. Lucy, his Border collie, followed at his heels.

Leeann pushed away from the corral and followed. Her brothers were all well over six feet tall and had long strides. She never had been able to keep up.

The driver's side door opened, and a man stepped out. He reached inside, brought out a cream-colored Stetson, and settled it on his head before turning to meet Carter.

As her brother greeted the cowboy, Leeann came to a complete halt, her heart skipping a beat. *Damn, what a man.*

He was at least six-four and about the same age as Carter, but the man was much rougher and tougher looking. She'd always had a thing for bad boys, and he had that look about him, sinfully sexy.

She swallowed, straightened her posture, and started forward again, her gaze raking over him. He had a trimmed beard and mustache—she loved men with beards. He was a big cowboy who looked like he'd be made of pure muscle, not an ounce of fat.

A jean jacket covered his broad shoulders, and he wore a faded pair of Wranglers that stretched across his powerful thighs. His belt was reddish-brown tooled leather with a big silver buckle. She wouldn't have been surprised if he'd rodeoed when he was younger.

Dear Lord, he's hot.

The cowboy greeted the Border collie as she walked toward them.

When she reached them, the man turned to her and touched the brim of his hat. "Howdy, ma'am."

Her belly fluttered. "Hi." She held out her hand. "I'm Leeann McLeod."

"Porter Gann." He clasped it, and the warmth of his callused hand heated her through. "A pleasure." His gaze held hers only a moment and he gave her a brief smile before turning back to Carter.

His hazel-green eyes were gorgeous, and that little smile weakened her knees. *Holy crap.* She'd never had this reaction to a man.

She checked his left hand and was happy to see he wasn't wearing a ring. That didn't mean he was free, but it gave her hope. She'd never chased a man, but there was always a first time.

Carter inclined his head toward the barn. "Applejack's in there." He tossed Leeann a smile. "The gelding my sister's horse. She keeps him here since she lives in town."

Porter glanced at Leeann before falling into step with Carter and heading toward the barn. Leeann trailed behind, enjoying the way Porter's Wranglers hugged his great ass.

She stuffed her hands into her jacket pockets and followed them into the barn, where Applejack waited patiently. He was such a good horse—she'd had him for six years.

"Beautiful palomino." Porter ran his hand over the gelding's golden coat and greeted him. "You are one fine-looking boy."

The horse whinnied and bobbed his head, and Leeann smiled.

After spending a few moments letting Applejack get to know him, he checked the horse's hooves. He turned to Leeann. "All four hooves could use new shoes. Do you want the one replaced or all four?"

Her skin tingled as he focused on her. She loved that he wasn't asking Carter since Applejack was her horse.

"All four, please." If the horse needed it, then that's what she should do. A side benefit was that the task would keep him here a while longer than if he was just replacing the shoe the palomino had thrown.

He gave a single nod. "I'll be right back."

She watched him go and fanned herself. "Now *that* is a man."

Carter chuckled. "Do I need to screen him to make sure he won't take advantage of my little sister?"

"Don't you dare." She playfully swatted at him. "I can do my own screening, thank you very much."

"Uh-huh." Carter made a disbelieving sound.

She eyed him. "And what's that supposed to mean?"

He raised his eyebrows. "Seems to me the last several men you dated we should have chased off."

With a groan, Leeann looked at the rafters and shook her head. "You five McLeod boys haven't liked anyone that me, Jill, and Haylee have dated."

"Until Tyson and CJ." Carter still looked amused. "Those girls finally got it right."

"Mind your business." Leeann sniffed and raised her chin, even though she was amused.

Porter returned. "I've got everything ready. Let's bring him out."

Leeann took Applejack by the bridle and led him out to Porter's truck. The back door doors had been opened. Inside was a workspace with a metal tool chest, a portable forge, and other tools of the trade.

"I'll leave you to it." Carter indicated the corral to the right of the barn door. "I need to get to work. Holler if you need anything."

"Will do." Porter nodded before turning to his truck.

Lucy trotted after Carter as Leeann called out to Porter, "I'll be right back," and she hurried to the barn.

Porter was wearing leather chaps when she returned with a small, three-legged stool. *Damn*, but those chaps framed his assets nicely. He set to work, lifting Applejack's front left hoof, which was currently shoeless. He settled the hoof onto a short stand he'd taken out of his truck.

She perched on the stool. "How long have you been a farrier?"

Porter kept his gaze focused on his work as he scraped and cleaned the foot. "Some sixteen years now."

"I've been around horses all my life." Leeann watched him remove debris from inside the hoof. "I've always found it interesting to see farriers shoe them."

He focused on his task and cut out the excess hoof wall.

"You're not from around here." Leeann shifted on the stool. "Where did you come from?"

For a moment, he worked on the dead sole before answering. "Montana."

This man wasn't going to give up anything easily.

She rubbed her thighs through the tough fabric of her jeans. "So, you were a local farrier?"

After finishing with the sole, he picked up a pair of nippers and started trimming the hoof. "I worked the rodeo circuit."

A light wind blew tendrils of loose hair around her face. "What made you decide to move to Arizona?"

He paused and blew out his breath before continuing. "You ask a lot of questions."

She grinned and braced her forearms on her thighs. "I'm hoping to one day make a living at being curious."

He paused again and looked at her. "And what do you want to do?"

Tingles ran over her skin as he focused on her. "I'm a writer, which involves a lot of curiosity and questioning."

"Never thought of it that way." He grabbed a rasp and worked to even out the bottom of the hoof.

"So, you didn't answer my question." She leaned forward. "How did you end up here?"

He sighed. "You're not going to give up."

She grinned. "Nope."

"My folks passed away several months ago, and I took in my adopted sister." He continued to rasp the hoof. "Ashley is sick, and we moved here to be close to her specialist."

Leeann deflated. "I'm sorry. I shouldn't have pried."

He met her gaze again. "No worries, Leeann. It's fine."

The way he said her name made her feel gooey inside. "How old is she?"

"Twelve." He adjusted the hoof on the stand. "Ash is a good kid."

Leeann cocked her head to the side. "I imagine going from single and alone to having a young girl as your ward is challenging."

This time, when he looked at her, a glint of amusement was in his eyes. "Who says I'm single and alone?"

Heat flushed through her, and she felt mortified. "I'm sorry. I just assumed since you've been going around the circuit."

The corner of his mouth quirked into a grin. "I am single, and I was alone, so you're right, it's a challenge."

He focused on the hoof again and started rasping the outside.

Males. Leeann put the heel of her hand to her forehead. *Heaven, help me.*

But she was thrilled to know he was single. He hadn't lived in the area long, so she was hopeful he hadn't found anyone who interested him.

"Has Ashley started school?" Leeann asked. "What year is she in?"

"Sixth grade." He released the horse's leg, and Applejack put his foot on the ground. "She'll start back after the holidays."

"The middle school is close to the hospital where I work." She watched him set an anvil on a stand. "The schools here have great ratings."

"You said you're a writer." Porter put on gloves and used long tongs to insert a horseshoe into the portable forge. "What do you do at the hospital?"

Wow, he'd asked her a question. Progress.

"I've worked there for eight years as an X-ray tech." She pushed her ponytail over her shoulder. "I am so ready to leave my current career and write full time, but it's like they say—don't quit your day job until you know you can make a living as an author. My goal is two years."

He pulled the red-hot glowing horseshoe out of the forge. "How many books have you published?"

"My first one comes out next month, the week after Christmas." She watched as he pounded and shaped the horseshoe on the anvil. "I have a three-book contract with a New York publisher."

He set the horseshoe into a metal container and carried the bucket to the horse. Applejack swished his long white tail. "You must be excited."

"I am." She smiled, feeling giddy. "I can't believe it's finally coming out."

"Congratulations." He picked up Applejack's leg and put the horse's hoof back on the stand.

"Thank you." She put her elbows on her knees and her chin in her hands.

Porter pressed the still-hot horseshoe against the hoof. Steam billowed from the contact, and he blew on it before removing the shoe. He used a wire brush on the hoof and then the nippers to trim it.

Then he placed the hot shoe against the hoof again, more sizzling sounds and steam rising from the contact. He set the shoe aside and did a little more trimming before moving the horse's leg so that Applejack could stand on it again.

While the horseshoe cooled, he started on the gelding's other front hoof.

"You're good at what you do." Leeann smiled. "It's clear you enjoy it."

Unlike the first hoof, this one had a shoe. He tapped on the metal before prying out the horseshoe nails and dropping them into a bucket with a clank after each one. "I like working with horses."

"Now that you're not on the circuit, do you do something else when you're not being a farrier?"

"I bought a ranch on the other side of King Creek." He tossed the old shoe in with the nails, and it hit with a loud clatter. "I have a small herd and the horses I brought with us. I'll build up the herd in the spring."

"Four of my brothers, Carter, Justin, Brady, and Colt, are ranchers, and one, Bear, is the town vet. Bear also has a small ranch with a menagerie of pets."

Porter remained focused on cleaning out the second hoof. "So I've heard."

She found herself fascinated by what he was doing—it was so satisfying to see the hoof transform. "What did you do last week for Thanksgiving?"

"We had a quiet holiday." He picked up the nippers.

Her holiday had been filled with her huge family and good times. She felt bad that Porter and his sister had been alone. "Did you have a big meal? Do you like to cook?"

"Enough for the two of us." He shrugged one shoulder. "Ashley likes to prepare dinner. I only do what's necessary."

"I like to cook." Leeann shifted on the stool. "I find it relaxing."

Porter's lips twitched as if he found that amusing. "I'd rather get a nail driven through my boot with my foot still in it."

"Ouch." Leeann winced. "That bad, huh?"

"That bad."

Leeann followed his movements as he trimmed the hoof. "What does Ashley like to cook?"

"Any kind of pasta is her favorite." He set aside the nippers and picked up the rasp. "She likes to bake cookies."

Porter seemed to have warmed up to her. *Score one for Leeann.*

She watched the play of muscles in his forearms. "Ashley must be a lot younger than you."

He rasped the bottom of the hoof. "Are you trying to find out how old I am?"

"I figure you must be in your thirties." She twisted on the stool. "All of us are, except Haylee, who's in her late twenties." She scrunched her nose. "Strike that, Carter's in his early forties now."

He adjusted the angle of the rasp. "If you insist, I'm thirty-seven."

That wasn't such a difference in their ages. She grinned. "I turned thirty less than a year ago." She thought about it. "So that makes you twenty-five years older than your sister."

"Yep."

Leeann tilted her head to the side. "What made your parents adopt a child who's so much younger than you?"

Porter blew out his breath. "You like to talk."

"I've been known to be chatty." She smiled.

He met her gaze. "I haven't."

She put one heel on the stool and linked her hands around her knee. "Now's your opportunity."

"God help me." He shook his head.

Leeann couldn't help but laugh. "Come on, it's not that hard."

He changed his position and rasped the front of the hoof. "Mom was close friends with Ashley's mother, Tammy, who was dying of cancer." He didn't look at her as he continued to work. "Tammy convinced my parents to adopt her daughter so that she wouldn't end up in the foster system." He shrugged. "My mom said Ashley kept them young."

Porter had just said more at one time than he had during their mostly one-sided conversation.

"What happened to your parents?" Leeann asked softly.

"My dad was a rancher, but he was also a pilot with a small Cessna." Porter set the rasp aside, got up, and went to the forge. "One day, the engine went out, and the plane went down, killing my parents and another couple who were with them. They were all on their way to Las Vegas for the weekend."

"I'm sorry." Leeann's heart broke for Porter and his young sister. "When did that happen?"

"A couple of months ago." He inserted a horseshoe into the forge.

Leeann frowned. "Am I asking too many questions?"

A glint of amusement in his eyes when he looked at her. "And if I said yes?"

She couldn't help a laugh. "It probably wouldn't stop me."

"That's what I thought." He brought out the horseshoe, glowing fiery red, and set it in the metal container he'd used earlier.

Before she could ask another question, his cell rang. He pulled it out of its holster, touched the screen, then brought the phone to his ear. "What's up, Ash?"

A crease formed between his eyes as the girl spoke. "You spilled red fruit juice on your white hoodie?" he asked then listened a moment. "Did you try the stain-removing spray?" He waited before saying, "How about one of those stain sticks in the laundry room cabinet?" After a moment, he blew out his breath. "Honey, I don't know what else to tell you to do."

Leeann spoke up. "I might be able to help, Porter."

"Just a sec, Ash." He lowered the phone. "I'm listening."

She nodded toward her champagne silver Nissan Rogue, parked next to Carter's truck. "This morning, I bought a cleaner that gets out red stains. I'd be happy to send it home with you."

Porter nodded. "I appreciate that." He brought the phone back to his ear. "A lady at the ranch I'm at now said she can send home something that will help. Why don't you put your hoodie

on top of the washing machine, and we'll take care of it tonight."
He listened. "See you in about an hour and a half."

"Ashley said to tell you thank you." He slid his phone back
into its holster. I'm surely grateful for your help. It's a white
Hello Kitty hoodie that she just got for her birthday, and she was
upset about the stain."

"You're welcome. We country folk watch out for each other."
Leeann smiled. "I'll give it to you before you leave."

Porter went back to work on shoeing Applejack while
Leeann stuck around. When he started on his rear left hoof, she
noticed the bottom of a tattoo on Porter's left biceps that she
hadn't seen when he'd been turned the other way.

"What kind of tattoo is that?" she asked.

He positioned the horse's leg so that his hoof was on the
short stand. "Roadrunner."

She leaned closer. "Can I see it?"

He glanced at her, then paused to push up his sleeve,
exposing his rock-hard muscular arm. It was an attractive tattoo
with a roadrunner and cacti encircled by a lasso.

"I like it." She studied it before meeting his gaze. "You're
from a state that doesn't have that bird or vegetation. How did
you end up with that tattoo?"

"Lost a bet." He pulled his sleeve down before going back to
work.

She rolled her eyes. "Isn't that the standard don't-ask
response?"

A smile was in his eyes when he flicked his gaze back to her.
"Could be."

Getting anything out of the man was like pulling a stubborn
mule's rope, where the creature had his heels dug in and could
barely be budged. But what little she did coax out of Porter was a
small triumph that made her smile.

Leeann continued to pry information out of him while he

finished each hoof. When he finally got back to the first one, he took the cooled horseshoe and nailed it to the hoof. Like the good horse he was, Applejack remained patient during the whole process.

When Porter got back to the rear left hoof, she saw the bottom of his roadrunner again. "Do you have any other tattoos?"

He started nailing in the horseshoe. "None that I can show in polite company."

She gave him an impish look. "What about impolite company?"

His lips twitched as he met her gaze. "No, honey, you don't qualify."

Ooooh, he'd called her honey. She gave him her wickedest grin. "Try me."

He just shook his head and went back to nailing the horseshoe.

By the time he'd finished, she'd managed to drag out of him, in short sentences, that he'd grown up on a ranch, had gone to a trade school to learn to be a farrier, and had rodeoed in his younger days. But she hadn't been able to get any real details.

Well, they had to have things to talk about the next time they met.

When he'd finished with Applejack, she took the gelding to the corral and turned him loose. She would put him in his stall in a bit—she didn't want Porter leaving before she had a chance to ask the man out.

He'd closed the doors on the camper shell as she returned. Carter strode toward them, and Leeann muttered a curse word under her breath. She couldn't very well hit on Porter while her brother was there.

Carter slid his wallet out of his pocket, pulled out some bills, and handed them to Porter.

"Wait." Leeann held up her hand. "Applejack is my horse. I'll pay."

Carter shrugged. "You can settle with me later, sis."

"All right." She turned to Porter. "Let me grab that cleaner out of my SUV."

She strode toward her Rogue, not in a hurry, hoping Carter would leave before she got back.

Leeann reached inside and grabbed the grocery bag off her back seat. She had picked it up to remove a red stain on a T-shirt at home. Tomorrow, she would run to the store to pick up another bottle.

She grabbed the cleaner and tossed the bag onto the seat. She shut the door, whirled around, and smacked into a muscular chest.

Startled, she cried out and dropped the bottle. Her gaze met Porter's as he grasped her upper arms and steadied her. The heat of his hands traveled through her jacket, warming her through.

For the first time that morning, she was speechless, her breath catching in her throat.

He released her and bent to retrieve the bottle of cleaner. When he stood, he looked at the bottle before meeting her gaze. "Thank you, Leeann. This might be a lifesaver."

She finally found her tongue. "No problem. Just follow the directions, and I'm sure it will work."

"I'll drop off the bottle tomorrow." He held out his hand. "I'll give you my number, and you can text me your address."

If she hadn't been thrilled to get his number and to have him drop by, she would have told him to keep it. She slid her phone out of her pocket, opened her text app and a new message, and handed the phone to him.

He used his thumbs to type in his number, and she took the

phone from him. She put her address in the message bar and hit send.

A moment later, his phone dinged, and he checked it. "Got it." He slid the phone back into his holster. "I'll see you tomorrow, Leeann."

Oh, my God. The way he said her name made thrills go through her belly.

"Tomorrow's Sunday," she said, "so I'll be home. Any time will be fine."

"It'll be early afternoon if that's fine with you."

She nodded. "Perfect."

He touched the brim of his hat in a farewell gesture before striding back to his truck.

Leeann found herself breathless as she watched him climb in. She gave him a little wave as he drove past before going to the barn to brush down and feed Applejack.

A broad grin spread across her face. Porter Gann had given her his phone number and was coming by her home tomorrow. Just maybe it was for more than returning a bottle of stain remover.

2

P orter drove home, his thoughts landing squarely on Leeann McLeod. She was beautiful as hell with coffee-colored hair and eyes the warm shade of whiskey. And hell, but she had a nice figure.

The woman had asked him more questions than he'd been comfortable with, but in all honesty, he hadn't minded her asking. He usually liked to work alone, and folks normally let him be. But Leeann had hung around, and he'd enjoyed it.

As for the stain remover, he could have offered to buy her another bottle, but truth was, he wanted to see her again. He liked her quick grin, her keen intellect, and the fearless way she spoke with him. He knew he intimidated a lot of women of her caliber, but Leeann had been entirely at ease with him.

His thoughts turned to his kid sister, and he sighed. Leeann had been right about going from being single and alone to having a twelve-year-old kid in his life. He hadn't known Ashley well, since he'd mostly been on the road and hadn't visited their folks often enough. Now that he'd spent some time with her, he'd grown used to having her around.

When he reached his new ranch, he pulled up to the house

that was too large for him and Ashley. But he liked it, and the rest of the property, and King Creek was a good place to raise a kid.

He grabbed the bottle of cleaner, left his truck, strode to the front door, and used the key to open it. He'd insisted that Ashley keep the doors locked. He'd been told it was a safe community, but she was young, and he couldn't trust that every person would have good intentions.

"Ash?" He headed for the kitchen, where he found her at the stove, the scent of Italian red sauce filling his nostrils. "Something smells good."

"I'm making spaghetti." She turned and smiled. "It's almost done."

The girl had the kind of smile that could melt an old codger's heart. So that went to say she'd certainly softened his own.

He set the cleaner on the counter. "Leeann says to follow the directions on the bottle, and it'll take the stain out."

"I'm so glad." She turned away from the stove and scanned the instructions on the bottle before setting it down. "I'll do it after dinner." She tipped her head to the side, her long dark braid flopping over her shoulder. A sharp pang went through his belly—with her new treatment, would all that hair fall out? "Who is Leeann?" she asked.

A sexy, beautiful woman, he thought to himself. Out loud, he said, "I reshod her palomino—the prettiest gold coat and white mane and tail that I've ever seen."

Eyes sparkling, Ashley perked up—she loved horses. "Can I see it?"

Porter shrugged. "Maybe one day."

He got out pasta bowls and silverware, and then Ashley loaded the bowls with spaghetti and sauce.

Ashley drilled him on what he'd seen at the ranch, and he did his best to engage with her. Bringing a kid into his previously lonely had been tough. It had forced him out of his comfort zone, but he'd do anything for her.

After dinner, and once they'd cleaned the kitchen and loaded the dishwasher, he helped her clean her hoodie. It took minimal effort to get the stain out, and Porter relaxed. That was one catastrophe averted.

"I want to meet Leeann." Ashley closed the lid on the washer.

"I'm taking the bottle to her tomorrow." He followed Ashley out of the laundry room and into the kitchen. "Do you want to come with me?"

"*Yes.*" She turned and nodded vigorously. "I'm so bored here at home."

He pushed his fingers through his hair. "Won't be long until you start school after the holidays."

She plopped onto a chair at the table, and her Ragdoll, Enya, came into the room and jumped onto her lap. Ashley stroked it, looking thoughtful. "We need to get a tree and decorations."

He hadn't even thought about that. He'd never had one while living alone. "We'll make a trip into Phoenix if we can't find what we need locally."

"What are we doing for Christmas?" She hugged Enya.

"We could find a place in Phoenix that serves dinner on the holidays." He shrugged. "I heard about a pasta place that'll be open—you love pasta."

"For Christmas?" Ashley scrunched her nose.

He slid into the chair opposite her. "We'll figure something out."

"I hope so." Ashley sighed as she settled the cat in her lap. "Thanksgiving was a little lonely with just the two of us."

"I know, kiddo." Porter gave her a smile, wanting to cheer her up, but he didn't know how. "We'll get that tree and decorations and do it right."

She returned his smile. "Deal."

He looked at the copper kitchen clock that came with the place. "Time to hit the hay."

Ashley groaned. "Can I stay up and watch TV in my room for another hour?"

"Since we don't have to worry about it being a school night, that'll be fine." He wondered if he was being too lenient or too strict. "But then lights out. Got it?"

"Got it." The girl pushed back her chair, and Enya jumped out of her lap. Ashley stood as he did, and she hugged him around the middle. "I love you, Porter."

Her words startled him. She'd never told him that before.

"Love you, too, kiddo." He patted her shoulder.

She looked up and gave him one of her radiant smiles. "Good night." She whirled and headed off to bed.

He pinched the bridge of his nose with his thumb and forefinger before raising his head and sighing. He was stumbling through this parenting business. Sometimes, he seemed to get it right. Other times, he flat-out missed the target.

That girl had him twisted around her little finger. He'd do anything for her.

What would Leeann think of dating a man with a kid? With all her flirting, she hadn't seemed to think twice about it. Women mostly mystified him, but she was interested if he read her right.

When it came down to it, he and Ashley were a package deal. So, she would be a part of his future plans for some time to come. He just prayed the specialist would have a treatment that would send the cancer into remission.

He headed off to bed, keenly interested in what would happen tomorrow when he and Ashley saw Leeann.

. . .

THE AFTERNOON FOLLOWING MEETING PORTER, Leeann sat at the kitchen table with her laptop and pored over her social media accounts. She did her best to focus on her new career rather than the man who had set her world on fire.

She didn't have readers or much of a following yet, but she'd been doing her best to create a presence on all the major social media platforms and promote. Thanks to Ellie, she'd been working on it since she got her contract. She even had a news-letter list that had grown with a lot of effort on her part and her cousin's.

Leeann found Ellie's name in her favorites and made the call. Her cousin, whose given name was Elsa, thanks to her German mother, had been such a huge help in navigating the waters of social media.

"Good morning." Ellie's cheery voice came over the connec-tion. "How are your numbers on Instagram?"

"How did you know I'm working on it?" Leeann sighed. "This is not my favorite thing to do—I'd much rather talk with people in person."

"Well, you can't meet everyone who reads your novel, but you can communicate with thousands online." Ellie always sounded so positive. "You're doing great, Leeann. Keep it up, and you'll have a hell of a start to your writing career.

"I don't know what I would have done without you." Leeann played with loose strands of her hair. "I had a personal Facebook account I never interacted with, and now I'm on five other plat-forms with author accounts. How does a person keep up with it all *and* write?"

"That's why you'll eventually need to hire a personal assistant," Ellie said. "A PA can do all the work that you can't fit in. You need time to get pen to paper to build your career."

"I just want to write." Leeann groaned.

"Then get to it." Ellie could be a bit assertive to her cousins and siblings, but Leeann didn't mind. She loved her cousin to pieces.

"As soon as I finish liking all the comments, I'll start working on book three."

"I can't wait to read your first novel." Ellie spoke with enthusiasm. "I've always enjoyed women's fiction. Are there cowboys in yours?"

"Not a one." Leeann laughed. "Heaven help me when it comes to that breed." Her thoughts turned to Porter, and her belly fluttered. "Speaking of cowboys, I met the hottest one alive yesterday. His name is Porter Gann."

"Oh, do tell." Ellie sounded just like she had when they'd been teenagers, talking about guys they'd had crushes on. "The last thing *I* want in my life is another cowboy, but I'm intrigued."

"He's Mr. Stoic." Leeann grinned. "Applejack needed to be reshod, so Carter called a farrier that Tyson recommended. O.M.G., Porter's hot. I sat and watched while I did my best to get him to talk while he worked on my horse. I actually got to know him a bit—well, not a lot, but it's a start."

"Did you give him your number?" Ellie asked.

"Better than that," Leeann said. "I sent home some cleaner for his little sister's shirt, and he said he'd bring the bottle back to me today. He gave me his number, and I texted him my address." She looked at her watch and saw that it was after 1:00 p.m. "He said early afternoon, so I imagine he'll show up soon."

"Awesome," Ellie said.

The doorbell chimed, and Leeann straightened in her chair. "I think he might be here now."

"Go get him."

Leeann laughed. "Talk with your later." She disconnected the call, scooted back, and rose from her chair. She closed the lid of her laptop and headed toward the front door.

A decorative mirror hung on the wall, and Leeann paused to

look at her reflection. Her dark hair was in a messy bun, with strands of loose hair around her face. She'd put on a little makeup but had done her best to make it look natural, and she didn't think she looked too bad.

She hurried to the front door, wrapped her hand around the knob, and took a deep breath before opening it. Cool fall air swept in, and she smiled when she saw Porter and a young girl on the other side of the screen door.

Leeann pushed it open. "Hi, Porter." She looked at the girl. "You must be Ashley. Why don't you both come on in?"

Porter touched the brim of his hat. "Good afternoon, Leeann."

She nearly sighed with pleasure, hearing him say her name.

They walked into her living room, and she closed the doors. She gestured to the couch and chairs. "Have a seat."

"We can't stay long." Porter dug in his pocket and pulled out a new bottle of the cleaner. "Stopped at the grocery store to replace the one you gave us yesterday."

The brush of his fingers against hers electrified her as she took it from him. Their eyes locked, and her belly swooped.

"Porter said you're an author." Ashley plopped down on the couch. "I've never met a real author before."

Being called an author was weird, and it felt strange that anyone would be impressed. She wondered if she'd ever get used to it.

"My first novel comes out the week after Christmas." Leeann smiled and sat in the chair opposite Ashley.

Porter took the recliner to her right, apparently realizing he wasn't going to be able to run off without spending a little time chatting.

"That's so cool." Ashley leaned forward. "What kinds of books do you write?"

"It's a genre called women's fiction." Leeann crossed her legs at her knees. "My first one is about a woman and her adopted daughter."

"I'm adopted." Ashley glanced at Porter and back at Leeann. "Porter's my older brother, but he's more like a dad."

Porter shot a look at Ashley, surprise written on his features.

Leeann smiled. "Sounds like you're lucky to have each other."

Ashley nodded. "We are."

Porter looked like he could have been knocked over with a feather, but then he nodded his agreement. "That's true for both of us."

"He said you have a palomino named Applejack." Ashley clasped her hands. "I'd love to meet him."

"I'd be happy to introduce you to my horse." She thought about it a moment. "I'm at the hospital during the week, but I'm off Saturdays and Sundays. Would one of those days work for you?" She prayed Porter would say yes.

"Saturday would be fine." Porter studied her. "We're on the other side of King Creek from your brother. How about we pick you up on the way?"

"I'd like that," Leeann said.

"You two could go out to dinner after we see Applejack." Ashley had a mischievous expression as Leeann felt herself go red. "You could drop me off first."

At first, Leeann was afraid to look at Porter, but she pulled herself together and met his gaze. "I'd enjoy going to dinner with you." She turned to Ashley. "You, too."

Ashley shook her head. "Nope. Just the two of you."

The corner of Porter's mouth quirked as Leeann locked gazes with him. "I do think my kid sister is trying to set us up."

"Is it working?" Ashley grinned.

Leeann still felt warm, but she laughed.

Porter continued to watch her. "I think that's a fine idea. Where's a good place to go in King Creek?"

"Mickey's Bar and Grill is popular." She listed places off with her fingers. "There's Gus's Pizza, King Creek Café, Black Bear BBQ, and Ricardo's is a nice little hole-in-the-wall. Oh, and there's a new place I haven't had a chance to try out—it's called the Steak-Out Restaurant."

Porter's gaze never left her face. "Your choice."

The way he focused on her made her feel like he appreciated her and was very interested, maybe even as much as she was.

"I'd like to try the Steak-Out." She linked her fingers in her lap. "It might be quieter." She grinned." It's likely to have fewer McLeods to run into than Mickey's."

"Steak-Out it is." He looked at his kid sister. "Are you ready to go, kiddo? You wanted to go for a ride this afternoon."

"I'm ready." She stood, as did Porter, and Leeann joined them. Ashley turned to Leeann. "Porter promised that we could ride to the Superstitions."

"Just to the foothills," he said. "It'll be too late in the day to go far."

"Maybe you can bring over Applejack someday." Ashley looked up at Leeann. She was short for her age. "We could have a picnic in the mountains."

"I'd like that." Leeann smiled. "Can I give you a hug? I'm a hugger."

"Me, too." Ashley hugged Leeann before stepping back, smiling.

Porter opened the door and the screen, and she stood on the threshold. She shivered as a chill wind swept over her.

"Get on inside," he said. "You're not wearing a jacket."

"I'm all for that." She nodded to Ashley, then Porter. "See you Saturday."

"I'll text you this week, and we can arrange a time to pick you up," he said.

"Perfect." Leeann gave them both a little wave before she stepped inside and closed the doors behind her.

Leeann felt giddy with excitement at seeing him again and thrilled that they had a date planned for Saturday night. Ashley certainly was a sweetheart, clearly interested in seeing her brother happy. Apparently, she had liked Leeann as much as she enjoyed the twelve-year-old.

She went back to her laptop, this time to open a new document and get started on that third novel. Maybe she'd even throw in a love interest, who happened to be a cowboy.

COUNTRY FROST COMING WINTER 2024

CHECK OUT THE "KING CREEK COWBOYS" SERIES *AT CHEYENNEMCCRAY.COM!*

ALSO BY CHEYENNE MCCRAY

~

(in reading order)

~Contemporary Cowboys~

"King Creek Cowboys" Series

The McLeods

Country Heat

Country Thunder

Country Storm

Country Rain

Country Monsoon

Country Mist

Country Lightning

Country Frost (coming winter 2024)

"Riding Tall 2" Series

The McBrides Too

Amazed by You

Loved by You

Midnight With You

Wild for You

Sold on You

"Sworn to Protect Series"

Exposed Target

Shadow Target coming 2024

Lethal Target coming 2025

Moving Target coming 2025

"Deadly Intent" Series

Hidden Prey

No Mercy

Taking Fire

Point Blank

Chosen Prey

"Armed and Dangerous" Series

Zack

Luke

Clay

Kade

Alex (a novella)

Eric (a novella)

"Recovery Enforcement Division" Series

Ruthless

Fractured

Vendetta

Save by purchasing Boxed Sets

Riding Tall 2 Box Set Volume One

Amazed by You

Loved by You

Midnight with You

Riding Tall 2 Box Set Volume Two

Wild for You

Sold on You

Riding Tall the First Boxed Set

Includes

Branded for You

Roping Your Heart

Fencing You In

Riding Tall the Second Boxed Set

Includes

Tying You Down

Playing with You

Crazy for You

Riding Tall the Third Boxed Set

Includes

Hot for You

Made for You

Held by You

Belong to You

Rough and Ready Boxed Set One

Includes

Silk and Spurs

Lace and Lassos

Champagne and Chaps

Rough and Ready Boxed Set Two

Includes

Satin and Saddles

Roses and Rodeo

Lingerie and Lariats

Armed and Dangerous Box Set One

Includes

Zack

Luke

Clay

Armed and Dangerous Box Set Two

Kade

Alex

Eric

~Romantic Suspense~

Deadly Intent Box Set I

Hidden Prey

No Mercy

Taking Fire

Deadly Intent Box Set 2

Point Blank

Chosen Prey

Recovery Enforcement Division: the Collection

Ruthless

Fractured

Vendetta

~Paranormal Romance~

"Dark Sorcery" Series

The Forbidden

The Seduced

The Wicked

The Enchanted (novella)

The Shadows

The Dark

Cheyenne Writing as Debbie Ries

~Shawna Taylor Cozy Mysteries~

Cooking up Murder

Recipe for Killing

Pinch of Peril

Delicious Death

Taste of Danger

ABOUT CHEYENNE

Cheyenne McCray is an award-winning, *New York Times* and *USA Today* best-selling author who grew up on a ranch in southeastern Arizona and has written over one hundred published novels and novellas. Chey also writes cozy mysteries as **Debbie Ries**. She enjoys creating stories of suspense, love, and redemption with characters and worlds her readers can get lost in.

Chey and her husband live with their two Ragdoll cats, two corgis, and two poodle-mixes in southeastern Arizona. She enjoys going on long walks, traveling around the world, and searching for her next adventure and new ideas, as well as building miniature houses, quilting, and listening to audiobooks.

Find out more about Chey, how to contact her, and her books at **https://cheyennemccray.com.**

Sign up for Cheyenne's Newsletter
to keep up with Chey and her latest novels
http://cheyennemccray.com/newsletter